In the doorway, Jenny saw a man, very tall and deeply suntanned.

'Matt, come in,' Morgan called to him. 'It's time you were properly introduced to your new partner.'

Matt moved silently into the room.

Jenny held her breath. Matt Davis. The *famous* Matt Davis. He was one of Morgan's best mercenaries. She knew his résumé by heart. Now as she studied his eyes, which glittered with a hard intelligence, her nerves skittered and her pulse raced. With his wide, oval face and jutting jaw, that strong nose and mouth, he was one of the most handsome men she'd ever seen! And he was being assigned to work with her!

Jenny did everything possible to hide her feelings and not stare at him like some lovelorn teenybopper. But how could she help herself? She was going on her first mercenary mission with Matt Davis.

It was more than she'd ever dreamed of…

Available in June 2003 from Silhouette Special Edition

Woman of Innocence
by Lindsay McKenna
(Morgan's Mercenaries)

The Best Man's Plan
by Gina Wilkins

Big Sky Cowboy
by Jennifer Mikels
(Montana)

Royal Protocol
by Christine Flynn
(Crown and Glory)

The Runaway Bride
by Patricia McLinn

The Marriage Prescription
by Debra Webb
(Colby Agency)

Woman of Innocence
LINDSAY McKENNA

SILHOUETTE®
SPECIAL EDITION™

*First published in Great Britain 2003
Silhouette Books, Eton House, 18-24 Paradise Road,
Richmond, Surrey TW9 1SR*

© Lindsay McKenna 2002

ISBN 0 373 24442 8

23-0603

*Printed and bound in Spain
by Litografia Rosés S.A., Barcelona*

To Gonzalo E. Abelenda and Ezequiel Caviglia of Buenos Aires, Argentina. Two young, handsome white knights who rescued us from Agua Caliente, Peru, and got us train tickets back to Cuzco. Thank you! Chivalry, good manners and kindness between North and South America are alive and well. You are both, truly, romance heroes of the finest kind.

LINDSAY McKENNA

A homoeopathic educator, Lindsay teaches at the Desert Institute of Classical Homoeopathy in Phoenix, Arizona. When she isn't teaching alternative medicine, she is writing books about love. She feels love is the single greatest healer in the world and hopes that her books touch her readers on those levels.

**SILHOUETTE®
SPECIAL EDITION™**

*proudly presents seven more fantastic stories
from*

Lindsay McKenna's

exciting series

MORGAN'S
MERCENARIES

*Meet Morgan's newest team:
courageous men and women destined for
greatness—fated to fall in love!*

June 2003	**Woman of Innocence**	*Silhouette Special Edition*
July 2003	**Hot Summer Nights**	*Silhouette Books*
	(3-in-1 including Lindsay McKenna's **Destiny's Woman**)	
September 2003	**The Heart Beneath**	*Silhouette Special Edition*
October 2003	**Ride the Thunder**	*Silhouette Desire*
November 2003	**The Will To Love**	*Silhouette Desire*
December 2003	**Protecting His Own**	*Silhouette Sensation*
February 2004	**Her Healing Touch**	*Silhouette Special Edition*

Chapter One

"Morgan, are you awake?"

"…Umphh…"

Laura smiled softly as she gazed at her dozing husband. Thin streams of moonlight filtered into their bedroom on the second floor of their log home. She could smell the scent of pine as a breeze gently blew the diaphanous white curtains beside their brass bed. Snuggling up against his back, she moved her hand in a gliding motion around his rib cage. Though the comforts of living had put a few extra pounds on Morgan, he still worked to maintain the strong, athletic build he'd had as a young man.

Placing her palm against his darkly haired chest,

she reached up and placed a kiss against his naked shoulder. "Are you awake?" she repeated.

Morgan stirred. He forced his lids open. Feeling Laura's small hand against his chest, over his heart, he lifted his own hand and pressed it against hers. "I am now."

She laughed a little breathlessly and kissed him as a reward. "I know you had a hard day. I should have talked to you about this earlier."

Morgan liked the feel of Laura's silky nightgown. The way it flowed against his nakedness made him very aware of her feminine curves. Moving carefully from his side to his back, he brought his wife into his arms. She nestled her blond head into his shoulder, her brow pressed to his jaw. Ever since her kidnapping years ago, the trauma she'd suffered, Laura had changed. Not that Morgan could blame her under the circumstances. He, too, had been changed when he and his wife, as well as their eldest son, Jason, had been victimized during the incident.

"What are you worrying over?" he rumbled as he pressed his lips to her thick soft hair. Inhaling deeply, he savored the sweet scent of kahili ginger that she'd washed her hair with earlier that night, before they went to bed.

Laughing a little, Laura eased away just enough to catch his sleepy looking eyes. Warmed by his sensitivity to her needs, she whispered, "How did you know I was worrying?"

One corner of his mouth moved upward. Her eyes shone with warmth and love—toward him. Squeezing her shoulder gently, he rasped, ''Why wouldn't I know? We've been married a long time. We know one another pretty well at this stage, don't you think?''

''Even at two in the morning you have a sense of humor.'' She grinned a little and kissed his jaw. The sandpapery quality made her lips tingle as she sank against him.

Sighing, Morgan said, ''Only for you, believe me.'' He'd lost count of the times he'd been awakened by a person on duty over at the Perseus headquarters about a mercenary mission. No, he savored a good night's sleep. Morgan also knew that since the kidnapping, Laura had kept a lot of her emotions in, and had lost some of her childlike spontaneity. Over time, he'd learned how to read her when she internalized things, and he tried to stimulate conversation with her, to find out what was going on inside that intelligent head of hers. Tonight was one of those nights, he realized. Laura rarely woke him up like this. He wondered if she was worried about one of their four children. Jason, their firstborn son, in particular, who was going through a very rough time the last couple of years as a maturing teen.

''What's bothering you?'' he asked quietly. He felt her hand range across his chest, her touch always wonderful. Savoring the feel of her slender, feminine body against his own, he moved his fingers across her shoulder.

Closing her eyes, Laura sighed. "It's about Jenny."

His brows drew downward. "Jenny? My assistant?"

"Yes."

All sleepiness left him as he wondered why Laura needed to discuss the woman who worked for him at Perseus. "What about her?"

"You know how much we both like her," Laura began.

"Yes..." Where was this leading? Normally, Laura didn't discuss business at 2:00 a.m. with him. She helped out occasionally on hiring people for Perseus. Otherwise, she had her hands full with their four children, devoting her life and time to them, not Perseus. "She's become like a fifth child to us," Morgan agreed.

The fact that Jenny had a lot of Laura's own traits hadn't escaped either of them. With her short blond hair and pixie face, Jenny looked more like one of their children than Morgan's secretarial assistant. Jenny had been abandoned at birth, given up for adoption, and she still didn't know who her parents were. When Laura had discovered that fact, she'd automatically extended a hand to the young woman of twenty-four, and made her a part of their extended family. Morgan didn't mind. Jenny was a superb worker, highly intelligent, and had graduated from Bryn Mawr in the top ten percent of her class. She had a degree in psychology, and spoke three foreign languages fluently. Jenny was no ordinary secretary, by a long shot. She was, literally, Morgan's right-hand person at Perseus. Everything that went on, Jenny knew about. She was reliable, trustworthy and hardworking.

"You know her birthday is coming up in a week? She'll be twenty-five?"

Rubbing his face, Morgan muttered, "Oh…no, I forgot. Damn… It's a good thing you reminded me." He made it a point to remember the birthday of every one of his employees. But Jenny kept the list for him, and knowing her as he did, he realized she'd never tell him her birthday was coming up! She didn't like to take the limelight or have anyone make a big deal over her. She was almost a shadow, a behind-the-scenes player in all respects.

Laura nodded her head. "A senior moment, sweetheart."

They both laughed. Now that Morgan was in his mid-fifties, he had found out that his memory wasn't what it used to be.

"I have a special gift in mind for her," Laura said enthusiastically. "And that's what I need to talk to you about."

Raising his brows, Morgan said, "Okay…whatever it is, get it for her. She treats you like the mother she doesn't have. You don't need my okay on it." He felt Laura laugh and she hugged him.

"Don't be so quick to agree, Morgan. The 'gift' I have in mind is unusual and does require your approval."

"You're up to something...."

She laughed liltingly. "You're slow, Trayhern. Must be the time of morning I woke you up."

He grinned and squeezed Laura, placing a kiss on her smooth brow. Morgan treasured these special moments they shared. They didn't have many, not with four kids and the demands of Perseus hanging over their heads all the time. "Why is it the man is always the last to know?" he teased back.

Laura kissed his cheek and then sat up. The sheet fell away and pooled around her hips. She saw the glimmer in Morgan's dark blue eyes and reached out and skimmed her hand across his massive chest. "That's why you guys needs us girls around."

Catching her hand, he pressed a kiss to it. "Okay, I give. What's going on?" He liked the way the pale peach silk nightgown with the deep V-neckline revealed her slender body. Even after carrying his four children, she was as beautiful and desirable to him as ever.

"I've been thinking..."

"Uh-oh...now I *am* in trouble!"

She giggled and met his smiling eyes and cockeyed grin. Despite Morgan's overwhelming work-load, when he was with her, he was more like a little boy than the serious, conservative military tactician that he was. With her, he let down his walls. He trusted her. He loved her. "Yes," she whispered wickedly, "I think you are...."

With a sigh, he struggled up into a sitting position. Leaning against the cool brass headboard, he held her hand in his. "Okay, what have you planned for Jenny's birthday?"

Laura lost her smile and turned slightly, her knees brushing against his thick, hard thigh as she met and held his glimmering eyes. The moonlight was bright, contrasting starkly with the deep shadows in the room. Morgan's face was square and large. Even in the moonlight the scar on his face stood out, a con-stant reminder of that fateful day during the Vietnam War so long ago.

"You know how desperately she daydreams of go-ing on a mission with a mercenary."

Morgan groaned. "Laura..."

She held up her hand. "Hear me out, darling."

Groaning, Morgan rumbled, "That's all it is, Laura. She daydreams. She knows she can't go on a bona fide merc mission. She's not trained for it." Scowling, he added, "Jenny is smart, bright, re-sourceful and creative, but she's not merc material. I can't put one of my men at risk to fulfill some romantic dream she has about this business. You know that.''

Sliding her hand along his jaw, Laura whispered, ''You're overreacting, darling. Remember last week, how you mentioned to me that you have a level one mission coming up in Agua Caliente, Peru? You said you needed to assign someone to interview Major Maya Stevenson's Apache pilots for that top-secret mission that will be going down in Mexico. Jenny's a psychologist. Who better to interview and help select the right three women for this? A level one assignment means no danger. Why couldn't you assign Jenny to go along? Make her feel like she's doing something important? Let her undertake the interviewing and choose the pilots. I really think if you'd do this, she'd lose her romantic visions of the business. As it is now, that's all she talks about—to be part of one of your merc teams.''

Groaning, Morgan closed his eyes. ''Laura…''

''Morgan, it's a little thing, but it'll mean so much to Jenny.''

Opening his eyes, he regarded her shadowed face and absorbed her warm, pleading look. She knew he wouldn't refuse her. He never did. How could he? Loving Laura was his whole life. Their children were proof of that, and their love had deepened and gotten even better over the years. She was his best friend. And she rarely took advantage of their bond as she was doing now.

Morgan knew that Laura felt deeply for Jenny's plight as an abandoned child. Laura had a habit of bringing in strays all the time. There was that stray kitten down at the grocers, starving, its eyes nearly matted shut, that she'd brought it home and nursed back to health. A pigeon had been hit by a car and was lying on the side of the road, and Laura had stopped and picked it up. She'd put a splint on its broken wing and nursed it back to health. Now that Laura had released it, the dumb bird made its home on the rail outside their bedroom door. Morgan wasn't very happy about that. The bird messed everywhere.

Morgan's mind ranged over the many animals Laura had rescued over the years. And he had to admit, if he was honest, that she had rescued him, too. He was a stray. He'd been abandoned in every way possible, yet, she'd opened her heart and her life to him, without question.

Morgan wouldn't make Laura beg. He respected her too much to play that kind of game. He saw that her velvety eyes were filled with love toward him. Sighing, Morgan squeezed her small hand in his large one. "Okay, okay! So who's available to go on this mock merc mission?"

Laura released a breath of air, leaned forward and threw her arms around his broad, warm shoulders. "Thank you, darling." She gave him a quick kiss on his mouth and said, "Matt Davis is coming in from Bosnia tomorrow. He's been on a level four mission, and I would imagine he'd like something a little safer and quieter.''

Morgan arched one black brow. "Davis? Baby-sitting Jenny? Oh, brother, Laura. That is *not* a match made in heaven. That's like putting oil and water together.''

"He's the only one available," Laura said, biting her lower lip in thought. "I've met him several times. He's very nice. Good-looking too. And single.''

"Is this all for Jenny's benefit?''

Laura laughed. "It doesn't hurt that he isn't married, Morgan.''

Giving her a dark look, he growled, "You aren't matchmaking again, are you?" Laura had a penchant for that.

Her mouth twitched. She saw Morgan's dark, assessing gaze on her. "Me? No. Go look at the database yourself. There's no one available except Matt. I'm sure if you explain to him the reasons for his being assigned, he'd go along with it. He's got a soft heart.''

"Humph. I've got to have a soft head to think he'd agree to it. I'm going to have to do a helluva lotta talking to get him, Laura. He's thirty years old and he will *not* like baby-sitting a rookie. Hell, Jenny isn't even *that*." Running his fingers through his black hair, he grimaced.

''Matt knows Spanish. And this is a Spanish-speaking mission,'' she reminded him. ''And Jenny knows Spanish. She won't be a problem. Besides, she plans all the missions with you and Mike Houston. Just because she hasn't spent any real time on a mission, she knows how they work. I think if you tell Matt why, he'll gracefully capitulate and do it.''

''I'm not so sure....'' Morgan wasn't. ''Grace is not his middle name.''

''More than anything,'' Laura said, ''please don't let Jenny think this isn't an important mission. Let her think that she's really contributing—that she's the best person for the job.''

''I can't let Jenny think we'll do this again, Laura. She's not qualified and trained in military maneuvers.''

Holding up her hand, Laura said, ''I agree. Tell her that it's her birthday and that you felt she could handle this mission. You can make it perfectly clear that there will never be another. I really think that if Matt gives her a taste of a real mission, without the danger being there, she'll quickly lose that romantic veneer she's put on mercs and missions in the future. Maybe she needs to go on a mission, experience it, simply to help her to understand the rigors and stresses on our people. It could help her be a better assistant as she plans these missions with you and Mike.''

Nodding, Morgan muttered, ''You've got sound

arguments. Maybe we *should* put her on a safe mission. I could suggest to Matt to ham it up a little for her benefit. Level ones are usually boring as hell to a merc.''

Laura sighed. ''You've got the right idea, Morgan. I feel this will work out to everyone's advantage. Jenny will fulfill her dream. You'll get an assistant back that understands mission planning more fully.''

Chuckling, Morgan said, ''Matt's the only one who isn't going to benefit from this trip.''

''Mmm,'' Laura murmured as she moved into Morgan's arms, ''Matt's a big boy. Somehow, I think he'll roll with the situation. Jenny is cute. And she's no dummy. He'll find out very quickly just how smart and resourceful she is.''

Morgan smiled, pressing his wife closer to him. As she leaned down, rubbing like a feline against him, he murmured, ''Let's set business aside now, shall we?''

Laura laughed gently and placed her lips against his smiling ones. ''I like waking you at 2:00 a.m. in the morning, Trayhern....''

As her lips glided against his, he felt her smiling. Her body was warm and sensuous as he wrapped his arms around her. ''Yeah,'' he growled, ''no interruptions...''

''No phones, no faxes...''

"No children coming in and needing something..."

Sighing, Laura whispered, "Just the two of us.... Let's take advantage of it, shall we, darling?"

"I need a special favor from you, Matt. Have a seat." Morgan gestured to the leather wing chair that sat at one corner of his massive bird's-eye maple desk in his private office within the Perseus complex. The merc, Matt Davis, assessed him critically with storm-gray eyes as he sat down.

"A favor?"

The door to Morgan's office opened, interrupting the two men. Jenny came in, bearing a silver tray with coffee, cream, sugar and those delectable Krispy Kreme doughnuts. They were Morgan's downfall. Luckily, Jenny had put only two on the tray—one for each of the men. Laura had given her strict instructions not to serve the usual half dozen anymore, or Morgan would eat more than his fair share.

"Come in, Jenny," he murmured. "You can set the tray on the desk here."

Matt rubbed his eyes tiredly. The little blond-haired assistant gave him a cheery good-morning smile, as she had when she'd let him in to see Morgan for his appointment. Her blue eyes sparkled with such life. She brushed by him and he caught the scent of a very faint fragrance; maybe lilacs? He dismissed his distracting thought. Right now, all he wanted was a week or two off and some deep, sound sleep. Still, those large, expressive blue eyes of hers got to him. They reached inside of his armored heart and touched him as if he had no defenses in place. Damn. How could that be? She was all of maybe five foot two inches, and probably weighed a hundred pounds soaking wet. She was built like a bird, Matt thought, and she looked fragile. Like she might break if someone glared at her or said a bad word in her presence. Yet she was all bubbly, light effervescence. Sunshine in their dark hole of a business, he mused. Maybe that's why Morgan had hired her: she brought light to the murky world they lived in. Matt couldn't blame him. Jenny was attractive without being a raving beauty. It was her eyes and that constant, soft smile on her full mouth that were her greatest attributes.

"Thank you, Jenny," Morgan murmured as she was about to pour coffee into the delicate white china cups. "We'll do it."

"Sure…" Jenny nodded and turned. As she did, the toe of her sensible brown loafer caught the scarred, dirty hiking boot Matt wore.

"Oh!" The cry tore from her lips as she staggered forward, off balance, her arms flailing outward.

Matt saw her trip. Instantly, he was leaning forward, his arm outstretched, to grab her. He was easily able to catch her as she reeled in his direction. In seconds, her light form was in his arms, her shoulder against his chest.

"You okay?" he asked as he righted her and sat her on her feet. Matt saw her cheeks turn red with embarrassment. Morgan had come halfway out of his chair when he saw her trip, but from where he was, he couldn't have helped her, anyway.

"Oh yes...sorry! I'm so sorry, Mr. Davis...." Jenny quickly leaped away from him. She nervously smoothed her tan slacks and gave Morgan a regretful look. "I'm *such* a klutz. I'm okay, Morgan. Really." And she held out her hand to stop him from coming around the desk. The look on his face was one of genuine concern. She loved her boss so much. He treated her as an equal, not as some dumb, airhead blonde.

"You sure?" Morgan asked, halting.

"*Very* sure." Flustered, she ran her fingers through her thick, short hair. "It's just *me*." Flashing Matt Davis a slight smile, she said, "Thanks for saving me from totally embarrassing myself."

Matt couldn't help but smile back. She was such a sprite. More like sunlight dancing on the choppy waters of life than an ordinary woman.

"Don't worry about it," he murmured, and reached for the coffee.

"I'll leave you now," she said and hurried out of the room.

Morgan picked up a Krispy Kreme doughnut. "You know, these doughnuts are the best in the world." He eyed it like a jeweler eyeballing an expensive diamond.

Snorting, Matt poured them coffee. "You eat 'em. I don't need the sugar today."

"Humph, I don't, either, but... Sure you don't want the other one?"

Davis grinned and sipped the hot, fragrant coffee. "Positive." He patted his hard, flat belly beneath the white cotton shirt he wore.

Morgan bit into the doughnut, a look of absolute pleasure crossing his face. "This is one of life's little gifts," he sighed as he enjoyed every bite. "When I heard they were going to have a Krispy Kreme come to Philipsburg, I knew I was in heaven."

Davis chortled a little and sat down, sprawling his six-foot-two-inch length out again, the coffee balanced between his hands. "Better you than me. If I eat bread products of any kind, I gain weight right off the bat. In our business, we don't need that riding against us."

Patting his middle, Morgan said, "I've got about five pounds here I don't need."

"Yeah, well you're in your fifties and I'm thirty. Big difference." Matt grinned.

Good humored, Morgan took the second doughnut and sat down. He ate it with the same slow satisfaction as he had the first one. "This will be our secret. Laura thinks I'm getting one a day."

"Our secret," Matt agreed with a lopsided grin.

Dusting off his hands on the white linen napkin from the tray, Morgan picked up his coffee and sauntered back around his desk. "Now," he murmured, "I have a favor to ask of you."

Chapter Two

"Happy birthday, Jenny," Morgan called to his assistant. He looked fondly over at her as she hurried into the war room, where all assignments were handed out. Laura stood at his side, smiling.

Jenny came to a halt in front of Morgan, who sat opposite her at the huge, oval table. Her eyes grew huge at the sight of the white frosted cake decorated with yellow roses. "A cake?" she gasped. Her hand flew to her heart when she saw the lit candles—all twenty-five of them. "You didn't have to do this," she said, touched. With a lump in her throat, she made a wish and blew out all the candles, while the Trayherns applauded.

To the left of the cake was a blue folder. She recognized the file as a merc assignment. On top of it was placed a bright red-and-silver bow. What stymied her was the fact that *her* name was on that file. Clasping her hands in nervous anticipation, she asked, "What's this?"

Laura smiled fondly. "Your gift, Jenny. From all of us to you. Go on, open it."

She saw the smile that Morgan traded with Laura. They looked like they knew the punch line to a joke she wasn't privy to. Anticipation wound through her. "B-but," Jenny stammered, gesturing toward the file, "that's a merc assignment file. Did I not file it correctly?" She took pride in her filing system and had never lost a folder yet.

"Yes," Morgan murmured in his deep voice, "that's exactly what it is. And no, it's not misfiled."

Giving them a confused look, Jenny slid her fingers beneath the bow, then carefully set it aside. Balancing the folder in her hand, she gave them a perplexed look. "It has my name on it. That's not right. The merc who's assigned this duty should have his or her name on it...."

Morgan allowed a hint of a smile. Jenny was truly confused. "Why don't you open it up and look at the assignment? I think a lot of your confusion will be put to rest."

Sitting down, Jenny placed the file in her lap and opened it. Her eyes widened. She gasped. Snapping a look up at Morgan and Laura, she whispered, "This can't be!"

"Why not?" Morgan demanded.

"Why, er, I'm just an assistant to you, Morgan...for Perseus...." She stared disbelievingly at the assignment. It had her name on it as the commander in charge of the mission. Below it was another name: Matt Davis. He was second-in-command. Looking farther, she saw that the assignment was to Agua Caliente, Peru, to a top-secret military installation known as the Black Jaguar Base.

Her heart began skipping beats as she continued to rapidly scan the information. She was being assigned to interview all volunteer candidates at the Black Jaguar Base who would want to work undercover for Perseus on an upcoming mission along the Mexican-American border. She was to lead this mission! *Her!* She was to interview all the pilots and then select the three she considered best qualified for the tasks. It was a level one mission, which meant there was no risk or danger to it.

Morgan traded a warm look with Laura. He turned his attention back to Jenny, whose head was still bent over the file as she read voraciously. She nervously chewed on her full lower lip, and her thin, arched brows worked up and down as she read. She had a very open, readable face, and Morgan enjoyed watching her response.

"Jenny, we felt that you've worked here long enough to undertake a safe, but very necessary mission for Perseus," he told her in an authoritative voice. Jenny lifted her chin, her full attention on him. Morgan saw tears in her eyes. He felt Laura gently squeeze his shoulder. "We know you've dreamed of going on a mission rather than just sitting here behind your desk processing orders and reports. I felt that if you undertook a mission, that would help you understand your job here better. And Laura felt this was a worthy birthday gift to you. Is it?"

Choking on tears, Jenny fought them back. Her gaze swung from Morgan's gentle look to Laura's proud and smiling features. She knew in her heart that Laura had engineered this. "I—I don't know what to say...."

"Yes will suffice." Morgan chuckled indulgently.

"But...how do you know I'm up for it? I mean, I'm not a trained merc. I have no experience in the military. I've never picked up a pistol to fire it...." She suddenly stood up, gripping the file to her chest, and her voice went off-key with anxiety. "Oh, I know I've told you a million times I wished for a chance to go on a mission...but I know better. I really do. I know I'm a big 'fraidy-cat, not a hero or heroine like the wonderful people you employ, Morgan. I'm a mouse. A plain, dull little mouse with absolutely no military background like your mercenaries.''

Laura smiled gently. ''Not all missions require military might, Jenny. You have a degree in psychology. We felt that you were the best qualified person for this mission. You've been here a year with us and you know the routine. And you've also met most of our employees and know the type of people we're looking for.'' Laura pointed to the folder Jenny held in a death grip against her chest. ''Major Maya Stevenson has agreed to let you and your partner come down to her base and interview any interested Boeing Apache helicopter pilots who may want to take part in these upcoming missions.''

Stymied, her heart beating hard in her chest because she'd never in a million years believed she'd be given a merc mission, Jenny said in a wobbly voice, ''But, Laura, I don't know anything about the military except what I've learned here. I wouldn't know how to assess the volunteers....'' She gave Laura a panicked look.

Morgan cleared his throat. ''That's why Matt Davis has been assigned. He's ex-Navy SEAL. He knows the military and he also knows what we're looking for on this mission. He can help you with the type of questions you might want to pose to the volunteers, as well as guide you in your selection. Of course, you are the team leader and he's your assistant. In the end, your judgment, your choices, are the ones we'll go with."

"Oh dear..." Jenny quickly sat down before she fell down from the shock of it all. What a birthday gift! Going on a merc mission. It was one of those silly, idealistic dreams she held secret within her heart, one she never believed would come true. Shaking her head, she muttered more to herself than to them, "All my life, I've dreamed of doing something heroic...something that would help others...."

"We felt you deserved this opportunity," Morgan said genially. He grinned as Jenny looked over at him. Her large blue eyes were huge with shock and wonder. "Will you accept your birthday gift so we can get on with cutting the cake?"

Laughing breathlessly, Jenny leaped from the chair. "Of course. Wow! I'm in shock. I mean, I really *am!* I never dreamed of this...oh, I mean I did, but I never thought my dream would come true." And she smiled bashfully at them. Putting the file aside, she picked up the serving knife and pulled a white china plate with gold trim from the stack at her elbow.

Chuckling, Morgan said, "You've earned the chance, Jenny. And you can cut me an extra large piece, please."

"Morgan," Laura warned lightly, "you're trying to watch your waistline, darling. Remember?"

Giving the white frosted cake a fond look, he said, "Just a little larger than usual? Chocolate cake is my favorite."

With a short laugh, Jenny sliced him a large piece. Dropping it onto the plate, she said, "Listen, you *deserve* a big piece for giving me this chance. I promise you I won't let you down—I really won't."

And yet, as she cut Laura a much thinner slice of the cake at her request, Jenny was already feeling deep angst. Could she do this? How? She'd never done anything like it before. Yet there wasn't a day that went by when she didn't yearn, heart and soul, to take off on a mission with a merc.

Oh, she had *such* fantasies! Most of the male mercs were young, in their twenties, and they were such good-looking men! Jenny, being single, had a tough time not staring boldly at them like a dog slavering over a nice, big, juicy T-bone steak at times. It took everything she had to keep her eyes on her work, remain professional and not stare like a love-struck teenager at some of the handsome hunks who came through the office.

Her respect and admiration for the women mercs, all of whom had come from the military, was equally high. They were all so poised, and confidence radiated from them like strong rays from the sun. How many times had Jenny ached to have an *ounce* of their self-assurance and poise? In comparison, she saw herself as little more than a scared mouse underfoot. They were all intelligent, too. She knew because she often, in her spare moments, pored over their résumés. The names of the colleges, universities and military academies, were a stunning tribute. Most had graduated from the top ten schools in the United States—a fact that made Jenny that much more respectful and admiring of them. And unlike her, these women were not afraid of anything. They were simply amazing, and Jenny wished many times she had just a little of their courage, their heroism, the guts and brains they had that made their missions successful.

As she cut several more pieces of the cake, she felt her foundation shifting beneath her like quicksand. And yet she had to look strong and appear as if she could pull off this mission. Above all, she couldn't disappoint Morgan. Or Laura, who often patted her on the shoulder and told her how much she was like the women mercs who came through their office. Jenny couldn't see any comparison. What did Laura see in her that she didn't see in herself?

Biting her lower lip, she looked up. Morgan was already digging gingerly into his piece of cake. Laura had sat down next to him and was spreading a linen napkin across her lap.

''Would you like me to distribute the cake to the rest of the office?'' Jenny asked.

Morgan shook his head. "No, you just sit down and enjoy your cake with us. I'm going to ask Roy to come in and do that. Today is your day, Jenny. Besides, you're no longer my assistant. You're a merc on a mission now."

With a smile she didn't feel, Jenny tried to sit there and concentrate on eating the cake. She tasted none of it, because her stomach was filled with fluttering butterflies and her heart beat erratically. Her emotions skidded from euphoria to sheer terror. Oh, what if she failed at this? She couldn't stand disappointing Morgan or Laura.

Roy came in, somber and respectful, and wished Jenny a happy birthday. She responded with a smile and thanks as she watched the tall, silver-haired man troop back and forth with plates in hand for the rest of the hard-working office staff outside the doors of the war room. Jenny saw a man, very tall, deeply suntanned, come to a standstill in the doorway after Roy had left with a final piece of cake for himself. It was Matt Davis, she realized, recognizing him as he scanned the room with storm-colored gray eyes. The very merc she'd tripped all over the other day in Morgan's office!

"Matt, come in," Morgan called, and waved him in. "You're just in time." He pointed to the last plate with a slice of cake on it. "Come and have a piece of Jenny's birthday cake. It's time you were properly introduced to your new partner."

Nodding, Matt moved silently into the room. He closed the door quietly behind him. His eyes smarted and burned. Right now, he didn't want to be here. All he wanted was twenty-four hours of uninterrupted sleep. "Yes, sir," he murmured, and turned toward the long, oval table.

Jenny held her breath. Matt Davis. The *famous* Matt Davis. He was one of Morgan's very best mercs—a level four. She'd known his résumé by heart even before he'd come to meet with Morgan. Now, as she studied his eyes, they glittered with a hard intelligence, making her nerves skitter and her pulse race. With his wide, oval face and jutting jaw, that strong nose and full mouth, he was one of the handsomest men she'd ever seen. And he was being assigned to work with her!

Jenny did everything possible to hide her feelings and not stare at him like a lovelorn teenybopper. But how could she help herself? He looked more handsome today than ever, dressed in a pair of comfortable dark brown chinos, a charcoal gray polo shirt beneath a buckskin suede sport coat and black leather cowboy boots. His hair, a raw umber color, was closely cropped in typical military tradition, and the conservative cut emphasized his rugged features. He moved like a prowling cougar across the room toward them, with a sense of tightly coiled energy surrounding him. His assessing eyes never left hers. How did he feel about working with her? Judging from the harsh slant of his mouth, he didn't like it one bit. Jenny cowered within herself, clutching the plate in her lap as if it were a liferaft on a storm-tossed sea.

"Matt, meet Jenny, your boss and teammate for this upcoming mission," Morgan said with a genial smile.

Matt halted in front of blond-haired Jenny. She could barely meet his gaze, she seemed so shy. What a tiny thing she was. He remembered her from the other day in Morgan's office when he'd come to Perseus to receive his next assignment. Hell, she wasn't a merc. Even now she was cowering before him and struggling to look confident. Her chin trembled, tearing at his heavily guarded heart.

"Good to meet you again," Matt rumbled, and he stuck out his hand. Jenny blushed at his reference to their earlier meeting.

Morgan had warned him not to make waves or let Jenny know he really didn't want this assignment with her. She was not a professional merc. She wasn't even in the military.

Jenny gathered her rapidly dissolving courage, lifted her chin and forced herself to stare up into those large, glittering gray eyes of Matt Davis. After all, he wouldn't want a coward for a partner. His hand was so large! she thought as he enfolded it around her petite one. Nevertheless, she accepted his firm, yet careful grip. Cringing inwardly, she knew her own hands were cool and damp with nervousness. His flesh was hard and warm and dry. He wasn't nervous at all.

For a brief, flitting moment, Jenny saw an unknown emotion glint in his assessing eyes. What was it? Disdain? Did he want to curl his lip because she wasn't really a merc? Not a military trained person, but a secretary fulfilling a romantic dream?

Anxiously, she searched his face for some sign of his true feelings toward her and this mission. She saw nothing except that one flicker of emotion in his gray eyes, which were focused on her. As she shook his hand, the plate containing her cake slid off her lap.

"Oh!" she cried. Leaping up, she instantly released his hand. In leaping, she misjudged the space and bumped into the table with her hip, tottering off balance. Strong, warm hands caught her by the shoulders, lifted her off her feet and set her down again.

Gulping, Jenny couldn't look up at Matt. He must be laughing at her. She was such a klutz! "Thank you," she whispered, completely humiliated once more in his presence. As Matt released her, Jenny crouched down to begin the process of sweeping the cake and frosting off the tightly woven, wheat-colored carpet and putting it back on the plate. Her flesh tingled wildly where his roughened fingers had touched her. Heat swam through her, and she felt a bit dizzy after unexpected contact with him. Matt had lifted her up as if she were a feather.

Laura came around the table and helped her pick up the rest of the errant crumbs. "Accidents happen, Jenny," she whispered gently. "It's okay. Let me help you."

"I'm so sorry," Jenny breathed apologetically. "I'm so clumsy...."

Chuckling, Laura said, "Don't worry about it."

Matt walked around the two women and went over to the sideboard, where a pot of coffee was kept warm. He picked up one of the white mugs in preference to the flowery china cups. Giving Morgan a sideways glance, he saw his boss smile slightly. Matt knew that look and that smile. It was a nonverbal order for him to say nothing—and to be kind—and patient with Jenny.

After pouring the coffee, Matt turned and stood with cup in hand and watched the two women clean up the mess on the carpet. Jenny was petite, like a fine-boned bird. He saw her hands tremble slightly as she got to her feet. Touching her flaming red cheek, she unwittingly deposited a splotch of white frosting on her face. Jenny reminded him of a rabbit—a creature without defenses, completely vulnerable. But then, Matt warned himself, no woman was defenseless. He'd learned that lesson the hard way.

Jenny rushed out of the room and down the hall

to the rest room, where she dampened some paper towels. Matt Davis was so tall, so strong and silent. She could feel him watching her every move. Oh, why had she wished for a mission? This was just awful. She'd embarrassed herself in front of everyone, when she desperately wanted them to think she was in command of her life and confident. Now she looked like the bumbling klutz she'd been all her life. Matt wouldn't respect her for that. Not at all.

Reentering the room, she saw that Laura had sat back down next to Morgan. She was smiling maternally toward her, and it made Jenny feel a tad better. But not much. Morgan gave her a look that said: *relax.* Matt was looking at her as if she was an alien that had stepped off another planet. She felt like a bug beneath his dark gray microscope gaze. What must he think of her? He had to be silently laughing at her.

Getting down on her hands and knees, she scrubbed the frosting off the carpet. To her surprise, she saw a pair of thick, chino-clad thighs sink down very close to her—Matt, crouching beside her.

"Here, you missed a spot."

His deep voice vibrated through her as Jenny rocked back on her heels to meet his gaze. Wet paper towels clutched in her hands, she looked up…up into warm gray eyes that made her feel suddenly weak and wonderful. When he used his callused thumb to brush away a smudge of frosting from her left cheek, she inhaled sharply, not expecting this kind of intimacy or care from him. A tender smile lurked at the corners of his mouth as he held up the offending frosting on his thumb.

"Oh…dear…it's all over me, too…" Great! She couldn't even say anything intelligent, much less coherent. She sounded like a breathless, starstruck teenager who'd been touched by her Hollywood idol. Well, hadn't she been? Hadn't she had a crush for Matt Davis for the whole year she'd been here? Yes…but the three times he'd come to her desk for assignment details, he'd treated her coolly, without smiling. Certainly, he hadn't recognized her as a flesh and blood person sitting behind that desk. And the other day she'd practically landed in his lap!

Now, he seemed different. She saw the amusement, the warmth lingering in his eyes as he held his thumb up with the offending white frosting on it. Heat soared up her neck into her face.

"That came off me?" How had it gotten here? Her mind whirled. She was blathering, something she did when she was truly stressed. She was making an utter fool of herself in front of her boss and Matt. Jenny wanted to disappear into thin air.

It didn't happened.

"I admit you're a beautiful birthday girl, but I don't think you need this frosting." Matt gave her a slight, one-cornered smile because he could see how mortified Jenny had become. She was as red as the worst sunburn he'd ever seen. Her blue eyes, luminous and huge, reflected fear, humiliation and embarrassment at his gesture. And where had his words come from? He wasn't given to making compliments toward women. The sky blue of her eyes seemed to become dappled with gold flecks as his words registered with her. For the first time, Matt saw a tinge of hope mingle with the terror and humiliation in her eyes. It was just a simple compliment, no big deal. But he could see it affected her profoundly.

Licking his thumb, he tasted the sweet frosting. Then he grinned a little to try and relieve her of her embarrassment. "See? All gone. Not bad tasting, either." Getting to his feet, he held his hand down toward her. Jenny looked at it woodenly. She appeared frozen by his gallant gesture. When she lifted her chin and gazed up at him, he was once again struck by the childlike trust that emanated from her. Yet she was a twenty-five-year-old woman. And she'd always conducted herself with prim efficiency as Morgan's assistant. Today he was seeing a completely new side to her.

"I don't bite."

Jenny grimaced. Her hand shot out and she gripped his callused fingers. With ease, he brought her to her feet. Instantly, she pulled her hand from his, as if burned. Gripping the wet, sticky paper towels, she whispered unsteadily to all of them, "Excuse me. Let me go get rid of these. I've got to wash my hands…. I'll be right back.''

Matt raised his thick eyebrows as the door shut. He cast a questioning look at Morgan. ''Are you *sure* you want her heading up this mission?''

''I'm positive, Matt. Sit down and have some cake. Jenny's just rattled, is all. She'll settle down if you give her some space.''

Laura cleared her throat and got Matt's attention. ''Be kind to her, Matt. Jenny is a wonderful, open and helpful person. I feel if you can gently guide her, she'll do just fine on this interview mission.''

Reaching for the slice of cake on the plate, he picked up a fork and said, ''This is like baby-sitting my kid sister—not that I ever had one. Jenny's clumsy. And she gets rattled too easily.''

Frowning, Laura said, ''I know this isn't the kind of mission you wanted, Matt, but you were the only merc available. Jenny is an open book. She gets her feelings hurt very easily, and she's supersensitive. She reads body language like a pro.''

''Great,'' he muttered, eating the cake. Not only would he have to watch what he said to her, he'd have to carefully mask his reactions as well.

''There's no danger to this mission,'' Morgan noted. ''You can sort of consider it a minivacation to Peru. Enjoy the country and its people. Just be there for Jenny, support her and let her know she can handle it.''

"Well," Matt drawled as he took another forkful of cake, "at least she's nothing like my shark of an ex-wife." His mouth twisted downward. "At least I'm saved from that on this mission."

Chapter Three

Matt tried to ignore Jenny, who wriggled like a happy puppy next to him in the first-class section of the Condor Airlines flight they were on. They'd taken a local hop from Montana over to Seattle, Washington, and gotten the international flight down to Lima from there. Jenny reminded him of the frothy, bubbly champagne. And as if sensing he didn't want to talk, she tried her best not to engage him too often in conversation. Instead she focused her attention on her laptop computer, creating questions for her interviews.

Feigning sleep, he had his eyes closed, wrapped his massive arms across his chest and spread out his

long legs. Even though there was a wide arm between the tobacco-colored leather seats, he could
feel her restlessness. Oh, maybe he was being too
harsh toward her. Jenny was in constant movement.
Maybe like a butterfly instead of a wriggly puppy.
Yes, she was definitely butterfly material. Laughing
to himself, Matt derided his protective instincts,
which made him want to reach out and soothe
Jenny's fractious, ongoing state. She was almost
manic. In the airport she had clutched her large,
black leather briefcase as if someone was going to
steal it from her. Matt had tried to reassure her that
this was a level one mission, and no bad guy was
going to come out of nowhere to swipe it from her.
She'd given him a dirty look that said she didn't
believe him.

The corners of his mouth lifted. Jenny was on
high alert as they passed through each airport facil-
ity, always looking about and studying people
around her as if one of them might be "the enemy."
Matt didn't have the heart to tell her that wasn't the
way spies worked. This was her fantasy—being on
a dangerous, undercover mission. Let her have it.
Still, he couldn't remove that warmth that was lingering stubbornly around his heart every time he
thought of her and her clumsiness or her breathy
laughter. Her delft-blue eyes shone with such life.
He wondered obliquely how someone like her, at
age twenty-five, had escaped all of life's hard
knocks.

She behaved as if the world were a wonderful place to be and live in. It wasn't, of course. Never had been. Never would be.

"Mr. Davis? Are you asleep?"

He stifled a chuckle as he felt Jenny's tentative tap on his upper arm. Prying one eye open, he looked at her.

"I'm not now," he rumbled.

"I, uh…well, I thought I'd like to discuss the upcoming interviews with the Apache helicopter pilots." He was looking at her as if she was a bug to be flicked off because he was bothering her. Gulping, Jenny mustered her courage and swept her hand toward the tray in front of her that held her computer. "I'm not in the military," she said, keeping her voice very low so they couldn't be overheard. No telling who might be sitting in front, beside or behind them. Glancing around and giving everyone a suspicious look, she leaned toward Matt as he opened both his eyes and uncrossed his arms.

"I just feel…well, really *awkward* about heading up this mission, Mr. Davis. I know I'm not military, and yet, Morgan wants me to interview the military pilots down there." She gave him a frown. "Over the past two hours I've been putting together some questions we might ask them. I really need your input. I'm nervous about this and don't want to mess it up." Jenny gave a short, insecure laugh. "And believe me, I can screw things up royally. If you could just take a peek at my questions?''

She picked up one page of handwritten questions and waved it in his direction. She saw his brows dip. He sat up and rubbed his face savagely. Jenny cowered inwardly, knowing he was tired. But in five hours they'd be landing in Lima, and she didn't want to try and formulate her interview questions then. She'd be tired by that time!

Matt looked at the tray in front of her. It was filled with neat piles of handwritten notes beside her laptop. Looking down, he saw at least fifteen wadded-up pieces of paper, like popcorn balls, littering the area around her small, dainty feet. Trying not to smile, he saw that she'd pushed off her practical dark brown shoes. For the flight she had dressed in a dark purple silk suit that brought out the color of her eyes and her burnished gold hair. Now he saw she had a pair of dark purple cotton socks on her feet. He'd meant to tell her how pretty she looked, especially with the dainty gold-and-amethyst earrings and matching choker, which held a teardrop-shaped amethyst pendant around her slender throat. With little effort, she looked both professional and feminine at the same time.

''Let's see what you've come up with,'' he muttered.

The male flight attendant came by and asked if they'd like anything to drink. Both said no.

Jenny sat there chewing on her lower lip, her eyes flicking from Matt's hard, unreadable face to his compressed mouth. He had a beautifully shaped mouth. She sighed inwardly and tried to contain the excitement and trepidation she felt as he went over her questions. Moving restlessly in the seat, she could barely contain herself.

"Well?" she ventured, concealed fear in her tone. "I know they're probably pretty awful, being that I've never been in the military...."

Glancing at her, Matt saw the worry and anxiety written all over her oval face. Such angst in someone her age...what had set her up to respond like this? Had she been overly criticized in her family? Had her parents been perfectionists when she was a child? Even the way Jenny held herself, so erect and stiff, as if expecting a physical blow, made him scowl.

"No...these questions are good. They're insightful." He tapped the paper with his index finger. "I like the fact that you're asking questions on a human level, rather than a military one."

Gawking at him, her mouth fell open. "You do? You mean you like them? They aren't awful?"

Setting the paper down in his lap, he focused his full attention on her. "Jenny...may I call you that? Or do you prefer Ms. Wright?"

"Er...no, call me Jenny, please. I hate standing on formality, if the truth be known...."

Nodding, he forced a sliver of a smile for her benefit. He was finding out Laura had been right about Jenny's ability to read body language big time. "Fine. Call me Matt, okay?"

She nodded hesitantly. Old habits died hard. At the office, he was always Mr. Davis. Jenny never called any of the mercenaries by their first names. When she saw his mouth curve faintly, relief shot through her. Even his gray eyes warmed a bit as he looked at her. It was much easier to deal with than his focused inspection.

"Good," he murmured. "I need to know a little about you. About your background. That will help me to help you in formulating your base questions."

The sincerity in his voice shook her, and the earnestness in his slate-colored eyes warmed her to her quaking, cowardly soul. Jenny had never expected that her questions would be worthy of the interview, much less meet with Matt Davis's approval.

Choking, she looked at him in disbelief. "You...want to know about *me?*"

With a nonchalant shrug he said, "Why not? You're my partner on this mission."

"I see...."

"You know, for all your friendliness and helpfulness, you're a closed book."

Wincing, Jenny looked down at the handful of papers in her hand. "I'm afraid I haven't led a very exciting life…Matt, and I really don't want to bore you with my life story.''

Such a cream puff. And a delicious one. Matt stopped himself from reaching out to stroke her hair, which looked deliciously mussed. Jenny wore no makeup and the way her blond hair fell soft and straight around her face made her look like a pixie. She looked so young. Yet he saw pain in her eyes and he wondered why. ''Want to play twenty questions, then?''

She managed a weak smile. ''No, you don't have to dig. I'll tell you. But I warn you, you'll probably be snoring like you were five minutes before I woke you up.''

His brows raised. ''I was snoring?''

Chuckling shyly, Jenny said, ''It wasn't loud or anything. Your head was tipped back, was all. A person's tongue relaxes when they sleep, and I'm sure yours was up against your windpipe, which was why you were snoring.''

Giving her a look of respect, he said, ''You're just a font of information, aren't you?''

Touching her cheeks, which were heating up beneath his dark, unrelenting inspection, Jenny felt her heart beating erratically. Did the man know he could charm even the meanest snake with those eyes of his? She wanted desperately to drown in his warm gaze. Just the hint of one corner of his mouth lifting upward sent her heart soaring with unaccountable joy. When he smiled, that hard mask fell away and she got a look at the real Matt Davis. She blossomed beneath his attention, especially when he gave her that crooked smile.

"One of my foster mothers always said I was a jack-of-all-trades and master of none," she began ruefully in answer to his question. "I know just enough about a lot of things to be dangerous, I guess." Waving her hands nervously, she added, "I have such a problem sticking with one thing and finishing it. I'm a Pisces, you see. My moon's in Gemini and I have Libra rising. I'm full of air and water, and the two don't mix very well, so I'm always at odds with myself. At least, that's what she said."

Foster mother? Matt scowled at how nervous Jenny was now. He saw the worry in her eyes, and the way the corners of her soft, delicious mouth pulled in. "I don't know much about astrology," he admitted.

"You're a Scorpio!" She blurted the words before she could stop herself. Slapping a hand over her mouth, she gazed at him wide-eyed as he tilted his head and regarded her in the silence.

"You got my birthdate from my personnel record?"

She nodded, her stomach sinking

"I see."

Allowing her hand to drop from her lips, she said

in a breathless tone, ''Don't worry. The information won't go anywhere. I know Scorpio people want their privacy. And they don't like people who talk about them to other people, either. They're very, very intense. Very focused. That's why you're so good at being a merc. You're a natural warrior. You know how to gauge people. Your perceptions are rarely wrong, either.''

''I'm impressed. You almost make me sound like a good guy.'' He saw her frown and then shift restlessly in the leather seat. ''So what about yourself? How about your growing-up years? Where were you born?''

Jenny's mouth quirked. Her stomach tightened. She knew Matt had come from a very prestigious and rich family. He'd been at the Naval Academy and finished in the top five percent of his class. He'd earned medals as a SEAL during the Gulf War. He'd been the head of his team until he'd quit to come and work for Perseus. She also knew, from the personal history in his file, that his parents had been married for over thirty years: the Davises were a happy family, no doubt. Matt had an older sister, a medical doctor who had graduated from Princeton University with honors. Jenny's hands hands fluttered helplessly as she answered his question. ''I was born in Medford, Oregon.''

''Oregon's a nice place. I've often fished for trout up in the Cascade Mountains above that little town.'' Somehow, Matt found himself wanting to alleviate the tension around her lovely mouth and erase the fear from her eyes. ''Did you ever go fishing in Klamath Lake, which is near there? Or fish for steelhead trout on the Rogue River?''

She shook her head and looked out the plane window. The sky was a bright blue, with high, filmy cirrus clouds. ''Uh, no...''

''Not a fisherperson?'' he teased. She refused to look at him. Now her hands were clenched, white-knuckled, in the lap of her dark purple skirt.

Softly, she answered, ''No...I don't like hurting anything. It pains me to even think of putting a sharp hook into a poor, defenseless little worm. It has no way of protecting itself from us...what we might do to it. Humans are a lot stronger, and sometimes brutal....''

Matt scowled. He heard a lot of pain in Jenny's voice. In fact, he could barely hear her, her voice had gone so soft. Her face had drained of color and she was pale. Very pale. And now she was sitting very, very still. His gut crawled with trepidation. Realizing he was stepping into very raw territory regarding her personal life, he said in a rasping tone, ''Don't mind me. Sometimes I'm like a damn bull in a china shop. I don't know when to stop asking questions. My ex-wife will confirm my dazzling skills in that regard.''

Turning her head, she met and held his stormy

eyes. Once again, Jenny was seeing him without that armorlike mask in place. Now he was searching and unsure of himself. She'd never have thought *anything* could rattle the heroic Matt Davis, decorated navy hero. Especially something she said. Her. A mouse. A ordinary person who had never accomplished anything of note in life. Except to be a great assistant to Morgan Trayhern. And she had also gotten a degree in psychology. She was proud of that accomplishment, too. But it wasn't the same as saving lives, like Matt did.

"My life," Jenny began quietly, "isn't anything to write home about." Shrugging, she opened her hands and said, "I was taken from my mother, who was a crack addict, when I was born. She died when I was a year old. I don't really remember anything about her.... I was turned over to the state, and over the next eighteen years, I went through five foster homes." She saw his brows gather grimly. And she saw sympathy reflected in his eyes. Heartened that he wasn't going to make fun of her, or tell her that she was less worthy in his view, she added, "I guess maybe that's why I went into psychology—to try and understand myself. I was hyperactive in kindergarten. I couldn't sit still. I disrupted the class. They said it was because my mother was a drug addict. But I never touched drugs—never wanted to. After I left my last foster home, I went to Bryn Mawr and worked to get a degree. I had to do something to prove to myself I wasn't totally a worthless human being.''

She tapped her head. ''I still have ADD—attention deficit disorder. When I was a kid they tried to drug me up to my eyeballs, in an attempt to calm me down. I just have a different way of working and thinking than most people. I thought becoming a psychologist would help me…to try and figure out who I am…or what I could be…. Oh, I know I'm a scaredy-cat. I screech if I see a spider…or a snake.'' Jenny shivered, placed her arms around herself and made a face. ''I really do leap up on a chair if I see a mouse. I'm such a coward. After all, I'm much bigger than any tiny little mouse or teeny spider or other creepy-crawly.'' She sighed sadly. ''I'm such a mess.''

''There're plenty of people who've come from broken homes,'' Matt said. ''And they go on to make something of themselves in life. That's nothing to be ashamed of, Jenny. You weren't the drug addict, your mother was. You were the innocent in all this.'' Without thinking, he lifted his hand and gently stroked her small, slumped shoulders.

Matt's touch was magical. As his strong fingers moved across her tightly knotted shoulders, she closed her eyes. His touch was healing. She felt the warmth of his hand, the strength, but also the tenderness of his touch. Amazed that such a large man could be so gentle, she released a long, pent-up sigh.

Opening her eyes as his hand lifted away, she managed a sliver of a smile.

"You're being very kind. Thank you. I know you don't have to be. You're a hero ten times over. You don't have to put up with little people, like myself." Her mouth quirked and she avoided his gaze. "I'm sure you didn't want this mission with me. Oh, not that anyone's said anything...." Jenny lifted her hands. "You're probably doing this because Morgan asked you to. I know how he sometimes puts pressure on a merc, to get them to team with someone they've never worked with before."

Just the flittery look in Jenny's narrowed blue eyes made Matt's heart wrench. "Whoa!" he murmured. "Slow down, will you?"

"I know...I talk a mile a minute. It's that Gemini moon of mine. We Geminis blather all the time. People like me don't know when to shut up."

"I'm interested in what you're saying, but you're running along at Mach 3 with your hair on fire, and I can't get a question in edgewise."

Laughing, Jenny nodded. "Fair enough. Okay, I'll shut up and you ask what you want." She couldn't believe that he didn't think less of her because of her background.

As Matt sat up, the look in his eyes set her heart palpitating for no reason. Maybe it was his unexpected touch. She would never forget that wonderful feeling of his hand sliding across her shoulders. Even now her flesh tingled.

Looking down and studying her questions more thoroughly, he murmured, "For someone who has ADD, you've done a very nice, disciplined and thoughtful job creating these questions. Looking at your work, I wouldn't ever think you had attention problems."

Making a frustrated noise, Jenny wrinkled her nose. "I was so afraid that Morgan wouldn't hire me when I told him I had ADD. People like me often make a thorough mess of everything, Matt." She gestured nervously toward the notes he held. "My mind works differently. I see things—letters and words—differently from the normal population. I've had to retrain and reteach myself how to think and do things your way, not mine." She managed a small smile of triumph. "It was hard, but I really wanted to do it, to fit in, you know?"

"Growing up, did you stand out at school?" Matt saw the instant anguish in her eyes. Jenny avoided his incisive gaze and clenched her hands in her lap again. He was discovering that when he hit a painful nerve in Jenny, she would naturally assume that cowering position.

"It was *awful*,," she admitted softly, her voice wobbly with tears. "I was put back into a remedial class. A lot of kids made fun of me. They called me stupid. A geek. And it got so bad I just hid. I ran from them in the halls when I saw the cliques coming toward me to tease me.'' She nervously touched her hair. "I wasn't pretty. I was such a stick compared to the other girls…and no boy would ever look at me. They called me Fraidy Cat. That was my name in school. The boys would put plastic spiders and bugs in my chair, or they'd throw them in my hair, or the girls would drop one on my tray in the cafeteria…." Sighing, Jenny forced herself to look up at Matt. His face was thundercloud dark with anger. At first she thought he was angry at her. But when he unexpectedly reached out and gripped her hand, and she felt his gentle strength around her clammy fingers, Jenny knew different.

"Kids can be brutal," he growled. "No wonder you're so jumpy as an adult."

Matt didn't want to let go of her hand. He saw Jenny's eyes grow tender as he held and gently squeezed her damp, cool fingers. Every protective instinct he owned rose to the surface. With the pieces of information she was divulging to him, he could understand why she was excruciatingly nervous and flighty. Her ADD made her restless, so that she could never sit still for long periods of time. And he'd mistaken that for manic activity. It had never crossed his mind that Jenny might have ADD. Giving her fingers another squeeze, he forced himself to let go of them.

"Listen to me, Jenny. Will you?"

"Sure." She sat quietly, her fingers tingling in her lap. Oh, how she enjoyed his touches! Never in a million years would Jenny have thought Matt Davis, military hero, would have such a tender side to him. She felt like a wilted flower thriving beneath the sunlight of his care and concern. Her heart flooded with such joy that it took her breath away. Trying to sit passive beneath his scrutiny, she waited for him to speak.

"You know what? I like you just the way you are. It makes me respect you a lot more knowing what you've gone through." He tapped the papers in his hand. "These questions are excellent. They cut to the heart of the matter, reach the core of the interviewee. You couldn't create insightful questions like this if you didn't have intelligence and a very good grasp of the human condition. As a merc, I strive to maintain similar qualities because it keeps us alive out in the field. You've got the right stuff, Jenny. It shows here." He tapped the papers again. "You're very good at what you do. Even if you have to hang off chandeliers and do it upside down, what does that matter? What counts is the product. And it doesn't bother me that you're restless or that you talk fast. I like to hear your thoughts, what's in that big heart of yours, and how you see the world."

Matt saw her eyes widening at every statement he made about her. Then her face went rose-red as she blushed to the roots of her blond hair. "And as for being a 'fraidy cat, well, let me share this with you. I'm afraid all the time. The only thing that might be different between us is that I don't over-react in the moment. I try to handle my fear and keep thinking clearly through it.'' He managed a slight smile. ''Where we're going, there's going to be a lot of bugs and spiders because it's jungle. But my bet is that you can use this situation to work through your fear and try to keep thinking, despite how you feel. I have faith in you, Jenny. And you know what else? I think Morgan picked the perfect person to head up this mission. I wouldn't have been able to create the questions you have. I don't have the training. I'm not a psychologist. You obviously know people, know how to touch them on a very deep, core level.''

Choking back a lump that was forming quickly in her throat, Jenny stared at him. She was in shock. Finally, she whispered, ''I—I've never had anyone give me so many compliments all at once. Are you sure you mean them? You aren't just saying that because you feel sorry for me?''

To hell with it. Matt reached out and grazed her flaming red cheek with his thumb. Again her eyes went a soft, velvet blue, and he knew his touch had a positive and magical affect on her. It was impossible *not* to touch Jenny. And it had been a helluva long time since he'd wanted to touch a woman like he was touching her. Maybe it was her vulnerability that brought out his own vulnerable side, which he'd carefully hidden from the world.

"As you get to know me better, Jenny, you'll know I'm not the most diplomatic person around. I am honest, though. To a fault. And sometimes—" Matt grimaced "—sometimes my shoot-from-the-hip honesty hurts the other person unintentionally."

"Honesty is good. Truth never goes out of style." She nodded and looked away. "You really think I'm cut out for this mission? I've had such angst about it. I worry you won't think I can carry my end of things. I worry that you'll think I'm nothing. Worthless. And I worry that you think you have to baby-sit me because Morgan twisted your arm."

Breaking out into quiet laughter, Matt raised his eyes upward. "You *are* a worrywart, Jenny. No doubt about it." When he saw her wince, he added gently, "I can handle your worry. What you have to do is put to rest all those other items. None of them are true. I'm glad I'm on this mission. And yes, Morgan did twist my arm—a little. And no, I didn't think you had what it took until I saw your questions and got more info on you as a person. Adding it all up now, I'm very confident about the mission, and you. Morgan was right—you need to be in charge. I'll be here to support you when you ask for my help. Frankly speaking, I think you're going to do a helluva good job. I think you'll be able to pick the right three volunteers for those missions.''

Jenny sat there, astonishment flowing through her. The sincerity in Matt's voice and that incredible warmth in his slate-colored eyes filled her with a happiness she'd never, ever experienced before. He believed in her. And in her heart she knew he wasn't lying. Her self-esteem got a big boost. Because of his belief in her, she felt the first trickle of actual confidence in herself and the mission.

Impulsively, she reached out and slid her hand against his sandpapery cheek. Though he'd shaved early this morning, that five o'clock shadow was there, making him look even more dangerously handsome. She saw his eyes narrow instantly as she briefly caressed him. Her heart pounded when she recognized the look in his eyes: the look of a hunter stalking his prey—*her*. Jenny didn't know what to think or say. She'd never seen a man look at her like Matt Davis was right now—with desire. Blatant, raw desire.

A warmth stirred deep within her, and that took her off guard, as well. Now her whole body was responding to his smoldering, dark look. Egads, what was going on? She felt unsure of herself in so many ways.

Jerking her hand away from his cheek, she quickly tucked it back in her lap and looked away.

"I never expected this…. You're so kind and caring…."

It took everything Matt had not to sweep Jenny into his arms and hold her. Simply hold her. That's what she needed. She needed someone to praise her. To tell her that she was a good person, capable of intelligent work. Stiffening his arms at his sides to make sure he didn't do anything he might regret, he rumbled, "You bring all this out in me. It's you."

Chapter Four

Jenny tried to swallow her surprise as they stood in the office of Gringo Bill's Hostel with the owner, Margerite Kaiser.

"You're in room 35, Senor Williams. You and your wife will be on the top floor, with a complete view of the plaza, not to mention beautiful Machu Picchu."

A short woman with a cloud of curly black hair, Margerite smiled as she lifted a key from the box on the wall, her brown eyes sparkling.

Jenny gulped. *Wife?* Was that what the woman had called her? Frantically, she searched her sleep-deprived brain for this detail of their mission, but came up empty. They had landed at Lima at 4:30 a.m. and caught the first flight out to Cuzco, at 5:20. From there they'd taken the Inca train down to Agua Caliente. Now, as she watched Matt lean over the desk and sign a fictitious name, she tried to recall if he or Morgan had mentioned they would be traveling as man and wife. All undercover agents went by fictitious names, but posing as Matt's *wife?* And then Jenny remembered reading somewhere in the back of the report that Matt and she would pose as a couple, tourists from North America—Matt and Jenny Williams. She was no longer Jenny Wright, single woman from Montana.

"Thank you, Señora Kaiser," Matt murmured, as he picked up the key. He turned and smiled down at Jenny. "Ready for our adventure, darling?"

Blinking belatedly, Jenny realized he was using that intimate, dark tone to speak to *her.* "Why, er…yes. Yes, I am, honey…."

"Sounds like you two need some sleep," Marguerite chuckled. Looking at her watch, she said, "It's 2:00 p.m. I suggest you take a nap. You'll feel better after three hours or so of rest. And then when you get up, go over to India Feliz for dinner. It's the best restaurant we have in Agua Caliente."

Jenny thanked the warm hostess and headed out of the small office with Matt. The hostel was beautiful, in her opinion—three stories high and made from river rocks gathered from the mighty Urubamba River, which ran no more than a tenth of a mile from the main plaza, where Gringo Bill's was located. Even here in the lobby she could hear the roar of the river as it splashed over huge granite and lava boulders littering its path. Walking from the train station, she had watched the wild, frothing water swirl and bubble around the behemoth boulders. Now, as she passed a stunning oval planter filled with jungle foliage and fragrant orchids in the center of the lobby, Jenny was glad she was here. There was high humidity at this time of day and she was perspiring freely. In Cuzco, Matt had taken her shopping for some loose cotton slacks and tops to replace her silk suit, which she had no business wearing in such a climate.

Climbing the cobbled stone stairs to the third floor, she noted the colorfully painted doors to the rooms, each a different hue. "This place reminds me of a rainbow," she told Matt as they climbed steadily upward. Impulsively, Jenny skipped up ahead of him.

"This is a nice place," he agreed. Balancing their two pieces of luggage in his hands, Matt watched her run up the stairs like a graceful deer. Her hair, although straight, responded to the high humidity. Soft strands curled around her brow and cheeks, giving her a girlish look. Her eyes sparkled like deep blue sapphires, and he found himself grinning. There was nothing to dislike about Jenny Wright.

She was the diametric opposite of his ex-wife, who didn't have a spontaneous bone in her body.

Hurrying down the concrete passageway and reading the numbers as she went, Jenny finally spotted room 35 at the very end. Opening the door, she stood aside as Matt brought the luggage into the spacious, carpeted, L-shaped room. As she closed it, her heart sank. There was one queen-size bed in the room, and that was it.

Standing there, she watched Matt place the luggage on the bed and begin to unzip his suitcase. "There's only one bed," she said lamely.

Matt nodded. "When you pose as a married couple, there's usually only one bed."

"Wh-what did you do in the past when your partner was a woman?" Morgan always paired a man and a woman on Perseus assignments. He'd found that the two usually complemented each other, both providing unique and necessary skills to the operation. Just because they worked together didn't mean there was anything but a professional relationship between them, however. So how did they handle such a situation? Jenny wondered.

Her heart skittered at the thought of sleeping here, with Matt only inches away from her. She wasn't afraid of him, of what he might do. She was afraid of what *she* might do to him during her sleep! Even in sleep, she was restless and always on the move.

Opening dresser drawers, Matt deposited all his

clothes into them. "We slept on the same bed together. Why?"

Jenny moved over to her luggage and started filling dresser drawers on the opposite side of the room. "I just didn't think about this ruse of being married...what it would entail."

Giving her an amused look, Matt murmured, "Relax, you're safe, Jenny. I'll stay on my side of the bed, if that's what you're worried about." He held up a pair of blue cotton pajamas. "I even brought pj's, see? Normally, I sleep naked, but since you're along, I thought I'd better dress for the occasion."

Her eyes grew huge. She gulped. Matt decided to stop teasing her, and folded the pajamas into the bottom drawer.

"You wanted an undercover assignment. This is what it's like," he said, stuffing his empty canvas bag beneath the bed.

Busying herself, Jenny said, "Right...yes, of course, you're right." Her heart bounded. "I'm worried I might keep you up at night. I squirm in my sleep. I'm restless...I talk. Sometimes I sleepwalk...." She babbled as she quickly stuffed her three days' worth of clothes into the drawers.

"We'll work it out," he soothed. Matt went to the banks of windows lining two sides of the room, all opened to allow in the fresh, clean air. Below them was the concrete plaza, a long, rectangular school topped with a Spanish-tile red roof on one side, a gray stone Catholic church on the other, and the Inka Pizza Restaurant anchoring the third. Up the wide main street, which was littered with *touristas* from around the world, brightly painted buildings were squeezed together in an unending line, and looked like boxcars hooked up to one another. Untying the thick, dark green curtains at the side of the windows, Matt drew them closed so that there was a modicum of darkness in the room.

"You've got to be tired," he said. Sitting down on the edge of the bed, he unlaced his Ecco hiking boots and nudged them off his large feet. Well-made boots indicated to anyone who recognized them that he was a serious climber and hiker. Rich *touristas* always wore them here in Peru. It was like wearing Gucci shoes in Italy.

Jenny turned and stood by the dresser, her arms wrapped around herself. "I guess I am," she replied, studying him. Matt looked exhausted. She saw dark circles beneath his eyes and felt a twinge of worry for him. The flight had been long and stressful.

Matt finished removing his boots, placed his large, square hands on his thighs and looked over at her. "You guess? I'm ready to fall over. Come on, I'll share the bed with you." He lay down with a sigh, taking the space nearest the pale green stucco wall.

Chewing her lower lip, Jenny said, "Uh…you go ahead and sleep for a while, Matt. I'm a little too wired to try and rest right now." She hurried over to the window and looked down at the plaza. School had just gotten out, and children of all ages, looking neat and clean in their blue-and-white school uniforms, were gathering to play soccer. Their laughter drifted upward, and she smiled faintly. She loved children.

"I'll just go down to the plaza, Matt. If I stay up here, I'll fritter around and drive you crazy, and you'll never get to sleep." She smiled as she saw a group of five-, six- and seven-year-olds beginning to choose teams for the game. Their mothers, all in colorful native costumes, sat on the steps of the school, knitting or crocheting as they kept a maternal eye on their children. A number of elderly people had gathered to watch the game, too. "There're lots of benches all around the plaza. I'll just sit down there on one of them. I've got to come down from this trip. I'll watch the children and rest up that way."

He closed his eyes. "Okay, have it your way. You got the room key?"

"Yes. Go to sleep. I'll keep busy, don't worry." If the truth be known, Jenny was absolutely petrified of lying on that bed alongside Matt. She wasn't sure what she'd do tonight, but right now, at least, she'd been granted a reprieve. Hurrying to the door, she picked up her purse, and her floppy, wide-brimmed straw hat, and left as quietly as she could. Relieved that Matt didn't know why she was really leaving the room, she hurried down the three flights of stairs.

Gringo Bill's sat on one corner of the main plaza. As she walked down the sloping street leading into the plaza, Jenny noted the sky was a pale blue with white puffs of clouds here and there. She spied a green bench on the sidelines near where the children were playing soccer, and hurried to it, breathing a sigh of relief.

Looking around, she saw the magnificent loaflike, black mountain of Machu Picchu, thrusting its mighty nose upward, to a height of ten thousand feet. The sides of the black basalt-and-granite peak were covered with greenery—thousands upon thousands of bromeliads and orchids. Agua Caliente sat at six thousand, Jenny knew. She was glad that she lived in Philipsburg, Montana, which was near that same altitude. It made it easier for her to breathe, acclimated as she was.

As she sat down on the bench, a woman in a brown felt hat with a dark umber grogram ribbon around the crown joined her. Though the woman was little more than five feet tall, she was big boned and strong-looking. Her oval face and high cheekbones shouted of her Inca heritage, as did her ebony hair, plaited into two thick braids. She wore a red blouse embroidered with bright flowers and a well-worn, dark brown alpaca cardigan with white llamas on it. As she smiled and nodded deferentially in Jenny's direction, Jenny noticed that her front two upper teeth were missing.

Jenny smiled and said hello in Spanish. The woman brightened. In her hands were several colorful, hand-knit alpaca sweaters, obviously for sale. At her side was a little boy about four years old—too young for school—holding on to his mother's dark blue cotton skirt.

"Hola," Jenny said warmly to him. She dug in her pants pocket. Matt had bought a couple bags of hard candy in Cuzco, explaining that the local children loved getting candy from the tourists. Producing a gold-wrapped piece of candy, she asked the woman if she could give it to her little one.

"Sí, sí, señorita." The woman glowed and bowed her head, thanking Jenny effusively.

"Bueno, good," Jenny said, and handed the candy to the shy little tyke. His dark brown hand reached out, his black, buttonlike eyes riveted on her hair. Jenny figured he probably hadn't seen many blond-haired people down here, sure Indians comprised the bulk of the population of Peru, with their black hair and darker coloring.

"Tank u..."

Surprised that he spoke English, she smiled at the mother. *"Habla inglés?* Do you speak English?"

"A little," the woman said proudly.

"Wonderful. *Bueno!* I'm Jenny. And you are?" she asked the woman.

"Maria." She looked fondly at her little boy, who had now inched forward and was sucking furiously on the piece of hard candy. "And this is Daniel, my son."

Leaning down, Jenny smiled into the child's bright, curious eyes. "*Hola,* Daniel." She put her hand out to him. "Nice to meet you."

He stuck out his sticky hand, his fingers small and fine. Jenny gently shook it and released it.

"Here, *señorita,*" Maria produced a clean damp cloth from her skirt pocket. "Your hand, eh?"

Thanking her, Jenny wiped her sweet, sticky fingers off. "It's my fault. I gave him the candy."

"*Señorita,*" Maria pleaded as she brought her merchandise forward, "would you like to buy one of my fine alpaca sweaters? I knit each by hand."

Jenny watched as the woman carefully laid out the exquisite hand-knit sweaters before her. "They're all so beautiful, Señora Maria." And soft, she thought as she ran her fingers lingeringly across the fuzzy, brightly dyed wool.

"You would look very pretty in this one," the Peruvian woman said shyly, avoiding her eyes. "The colors go with your Inti hair."

"Inti?"

"*Sí.* Inti is our sun god. Your hair is the color of

him," she said, pointing upward toward the mountains, where the sun had just disappeared. "Gold hair. It is truly beautiful."

Seeing the woman's wistful expression, Jenny smiled. "I think black hair is beautiful, too." She reached down and sifted her fingers through Daniel's short, neatly cut hair. One thing for sure, the Peruvian people were proud of their children. Nowhere in the plaza, which was hopping with life, did she see one child with dirty clothes or a dirty face. Their clothes were clean, if threadbare, and their faces had been scrubbed until they shone like polished mahogany. There were no runny noses, no matted eyelashes or dirty, unkempt hair. Matt had told her that although Peru was considered a third-world nation, the people were very progressive. They thought everything of their children and family. Cleanliness was obviously a priority.

Daniel shyly opened his hand toward her after he finished the piece of candy, to ask for more.

"Another?" she laughed, and looked to his mother for permission. Maria smiled fondly at her son and nodded.

"He is the last of our babies," she told Jenny sadly. "My other two babies, they die. The water. It is no good." She patted Daniel's head gently, her eyes holding a worried look.

Heart cringing, Jenny sat stunned. "The water?"

"*Sí, señorita.* Here, we have no good water. They

tell us to boil it. But my other two children, both older than Daniel, they drank from the river." She closed her eyes and wiped the tears from the corners. "I begged them to always drink the water I had boiled. But they did not listen. Now..." she sniffed "...they are gone. I pray to Inti daily to watch over Daniel. That the poison water of the river does not take him, too."

"Oh, dear..." Jenny reached out and patted the woman's hand. Maria was in her early thirties, but already the hardness of her life had left her oval face lined and stressed. "I'm so sorry, Maria. I truly am." If she'd lost two of her children, Jenny was sure she'd look as tired and sad as Maria—or worse. How could the woman go on after such a loss?

"We need wells drilled here," Maria confided in a broken tone. "Wells, they say, will give us clean, safe water. And we are so poor.... But it would save our children's lives. I wish we had the money to make these wells...."

Anguished, Jenny sat there in silence. Daniel, who had now lost much of his shyness, climbed up into her lap to rest his head against her left shoulder, his eyes turned upward to look more closely at her golden hair. As she rocked the boy in her arms, Jenny couldn't fathom losing someone as beautiful and cute as Daniel. Looking at Maria's grief-stricken eyes, she felt her heart quiver with sadness for the woman.

"Well," she murmured gently as she reached out with her free hand and patted the knitwear, "I really need sweaters, *señora.* I have a good friend back home who would love one. And I certainly need one!"

Instantly, Maria's eyes lit up. "Yes? Two sweaters, *señorita?*"

"These are all sweaters for women. Do you knit any for men? I have a very dear friend who is *muy grande,* very large. Do you have any big ones?"

"*Sí, sí, señorita,* I do. But they are at my home." She pointed up the concrete street leading from one side of the plaza.

Jenny smiled. "Why don't we walk to your house? I would love to see all the sweaters you've knitted. They're so beautiful. I'd love to buy at least three." In the back of her mind, Jenny thought that Maria could use the money. She saw that her leather shoes were thin and full of holes. Although they were clean and polished, they were well past their prime.

"*Sí, señorita!*" Maria got up and gathered all her sweaters, carefully placing each into a bag before she slung it across her shoulder. She called to Daniel to climb down, but the little boy shook his head.

Laughing, Jenny rose and straddled Daniel's legs across her left hip, her arm around him. "I'll carry him, *señora.* Don't worry."

"You are sure, *señorita?*"

Jenny patted the woman's shoulder. Maria was shorter than she was, but strong and firm from all the work she did. "I'm very sure. Let's go! I'm excited to see all your sweaters."

Matt awoke with a jerk. It was nearly dark. What time was it? He groaned and rolled over onto his side. Uncovering the black nylon flap across his chronograph watch, he saw it was 1800, or 6:00 p.m.

The door opened, creaking and squealing in protest. He sat up, his eyes narrowing. It was Jenny. Her arms were loaded with goods, he saw, as she turned and nudged the door shut with the toe of her boot.

"I see I can't leave you by yourself. You'll buy out Agua Caliente," he observed in a gravelly tone.

Jenny jumped. She let out a little gasp. She hadn't expected Matt to be up, and was trying to be quiet about entering the room. Nearly spilling her cargo, she brought the plastic bags over to the bed where he was sitting.

Laughing breathily, she said, "I'm going to turn the light on. You have to see the gorgeous, hand-knitted alpaca sweaters I just bought. And what bargain prices!"

Matt smiled a little as she bounded effortlessly back to the door and turned on the overhead light. He rubbed his eyes and felt the sleep easing from him. Jenny sat on the other side of the pile of plastic bags and quickly began pulling out the sweaters for him to look at.

"You never told me we could get beautiful alpaca sweaters down here, Matt. Look!" She held up a dark burgundy one with red, pink and orange hibiscus against a dark green, leafy background. "This is for Laura. Isn't it breathtaking? Do you think she'll like it?"

He opened his mouth to speak. By the time he did, Jenny had pulled out a second one—a big one that was obviously for a man.

"And I found this one for Morgan. It's huge! But so is he. Do you think he'll like it? Señora Maria had five men's sweaters, but I loved the dusty gold, earthy browns and red and orange woven in this one. It looks like autumn to me. Does it to you? Do you really think he'll like it?"

Matt laughed. "Are you interested in my answer or are you going to keep asking me a hundred questions first?"

Grinning, Jenny said, "Guilty. I'm sorry, Matt. I'm just so excited!"

"I can see that." Matt liked her angelic smile, and her shining blue eyes, which showed every nuance of what lay in her generous heart. Her mouth, soft and parted, beckoned to him. *Hands off,* Matt reminded himself, groaning inwardly. Jenny wasn't someone to stalk and capture. No, she was a butterfly, a beautiful creature not to be caught and tamed. One could only watch it flit freely about on the air currents, moving at will from flower to flower. Such was Jenny. His butterfly.

"Well?" she pressed eagerly. "What do you think? Will Morgan and Laura like them?"

He picked up the sweaters, turned them around and studied them thoroughly. As he handed them back to Jenny, who neatly folded them, he said, "I think they'll like them. Laura, from what I can tell, wears bright colors. And Morgan wears a lot of brown and gold."

Sighing dramatically, Jenny collapsed with relief. "Whew! I was so worried, Matt. I felt so sorry for Señora Maria and her son, Daniel. They're so wretchedly poor." Her voice became strained. "You should see their house. It's nothing more than a few pieces of corrugated tin all jury-rigged together with wire. They sleep on a dirt floor. A dirt floor! Can you imagine? I can't. She was so kind. She made me coca leaf tea and offered me something to eat, but I just couldn't, Matt. I didn't want to take food out of their mouths. It was awful. I just never realized…. We're so spoiled. So rich, in comparison. My heart just bled for her. And she works all day and all night for her family. She showed me the alpaca yarn that she's dyed, for the sweaters she knits. She makes money washing people's clothes down at that smaller river that flows into the Urubamba, on the steep bank just below her hut. She works so hard! I swear, I'll never complain again when I've got to work a few extra hours at the office. I'll always remember Maria and her working conditions.''

''You're such a softy, Jenny Wright.'' He placed his hand on her shoulder and squeezed it gently. When she gave him a rueful look, Matt saw the tears in her eyes she fought to keep back. She'd tucked her lower lip between her teeth in an effort to stem them. ''I like the fact you're so deeply touched by these people.''

Sniffing, she shrugged and absorbed his warm, unexpected touch. Matt's face was open. He was, once again, accessible to her. The darkness beneath his eyes had dissolved and he looked incredibly well rested despite the long flight they'd recently endured. ''How could anyone *not* be touched by it, Matt? The Peruvian people are so friendly and kind. I just love them!''

''And so,'' he said, mirth in his tone as he forced himself to take his hand off her shoulder, ''you bought a gazillion sweaters to help her out, to put food in her family's mouth. Right?''

She gazed in awe at him. ''How did you know?''

With a shake of his head, Matt said in a rasping tone, ''Jenny, you have a heart as big as Montana.'' Looking at the sweaters, he gave her a wry grin. ''So…did you buy me one, too?''

Chapter Five

For once in her life, Jenny decided, she was going to display courage in the face of the unknown. As she showered in their bathroom and got ready for bed after the wonderful meal she'd shared with Matt at the India Feliz Restaurant earlier, she made a promise not to act like a nervous Nellie about sharing the same bed with him. He'd made it very clear he was going to be a gentleman. Besides, he wouldn't have any interest in her. She was a 'fraidy cat, someone he probably had a heck of a time putting up with, under the circumstances. His other merc partners in the past, all women, weren't anything like her, Jenny was sure. But tonight she would show courage whether she felt it or not.

Patting herself off with the thick, yellow, terry-cloth bath towel after her shower, Jenny worked on getting her courage in place. Matt had already taken his shower and put on his pajamas. But the idea of him going to bed naked was provocative. She felt heat sweep into her face. Why did he have to be so ruggedly handsome? And he was so sensitive to her needs. He'd made a big deal over the alpaca sweater she'd bought him. The pleasure that wreathed his face had made her heart pound momentarily. The crooked, little-boy smile that came with the discovery that she'd bought him a gift had made Jenny feel warm and good all over. She was getting to know the real Matt Davis, not just the heroic military man and mercenary she'd seen a few times at Perseus headquarters. Jenny liked having him as her partner, but wasn't sure what her feelings meant.

Between the challenges she faced tomorrow morning when Matt and she would be flown by one of the women Apache pilots to the secret Black Jaguar Base to begin the interviews, and the idea of sleeping in the same bed with Matt Davis tonight, Jenny was feeling pretty stressed.

"Come on, 'fraidy cat, get your stuff in order," she told herself sternly under her breath as she shimmied into her pale green, silk nightgown. Running her fingers through her damp hair, Jenny peeked her head cautiously out the door. Thank goodness Matt had shut off the overhead light. He must have sensed her trepidation. The glow of soft sulphur lighting in the plaza below filtered into the room from behind the curtains.

Hurrying across the carpeted expanse, she saw that Matt had pulled back the sheet and light blanket on her half of the bed. Her heart began to pound. He was lying with his back toward her, facing the wall. The pillow was bunched beneath his head and jammed into position by his arm and hand. Gulping, she slid into the bed as quietly as possible. Lying down, she hugged her edge of the bed and brought the sheet up to her shoulders. It was fairly warm in the room. Matt had told Jenny that the temperature never got below fifty-five degrees Fahrenheit at any time because they were in the jungle.

"Good night, Matt," she whispered off-key. Her heart thudded with anticipation. With desire.

"See you in the morning, Jenny. Get a good night's sleep."

His deep voice soothed her anxiety. Releasing a pent-up sigh, she closed her eyes. Below, in the plaza, she could hear the kids still playing, even though it was 9:00 p.m. Maria had told her that most parents made their children come home about that time, so she knew the plaza would soon quiet down for the night.

She could hear the deep, continuous roar of the mighty Urubamba River, which ran between Machu

Picchu and Agua Caliente. Somehow the wild, rushing sound soothed her, too.

Very soon, Jenny fell into an exhausted asleep.

Matt jerked awake. What was that sound? He half
turned onto his back from his side. His arm struck
something warm and soft. Instantly, he froze. Again
he heard that mewing sound. Blinking his eyes several times, he moved quietly so that he was on his
left side, facing Jenny. The sound was coming from
her. Frowning, he eased himself up on his elbow.

In the plaza light filtering around the edges of the
curtains, he saw that she lay on her side, facing him,
and that she was literally scrunched up in a fetal
position. Her expression was tense. Her face muscles were taut, her soft mouth a tortured line. Gazing
at her hands, which were opening and closing restlessly against her pillow, he heard her whimper
again. The sounds were soft, but heartrending. Was
she having a nightmare? Matt fought the urge to
reach out and slide his fingers through the unruly
gold hair that framed her face. She moved frac-
tiously. One moment she was on her back, her
mouth working. Then she flung herself on her left
side. Again, a whimper.

He remembered what she had told him about her
life as a child, growing up. Jenny had never had any
real security, no real sense of safety, he realized.
Because she had ADD, she had been labeled a prob-

lem child to boot. He could imagine her several sets of foster parents shuffling her off to another home because she was simply too much to handle. Shaking his head, Matt felt anger. Didn't they realize that foisting her off on someone else was sending her a loud, clear message that she wasn't lovable? That she wasn't worth sticking it out with, or worthy of the help she needed to adjust to life and its demands? The thread of anger wound through his gut and into his heart.

Jenny flung herself onto her back again. And then rolled over on her right side.

Was this how she slept every night? Fitfully? Restlessly? Matt shook his head. She looked so vulnerable and helpless in that green silk nightgown, the boat neck decorated with bits of white lace. Lying back down, his hands behind his head, he sighed. What he wanted to do was sweep her into his arms and hold her. He knew he could give her that security, that sense of safety she wanted. Every emotion was so obvious on her face. Matt knew his touch could soothe her. His heart expanded with the need to touch her.

Shaking his head, he closed his eyes. *No.* He couldn't get involved with a woman again. His ex-wife had burned him badly enough to make him swear off women forever. And yet this small, feisty woman with sun-gold hair and eyes as big as a Montana sky made him long for a mate once more. Was he crazy? He was, no doubt.

He had no idea if Jenny would be well rested tomorrow morning or not. But he had to be. Rolling over on his side, his back to her, he shut his eyes and ordered himself to go to sleep. Tomorrow would come soon enough and a whole new set of demands would be placed on them. He wasn't worried for himself, but was concerned for Jenny. He wanted her to be successful on this mission because it would raise her self-esteem and give her a lot more confidence in herself. No one wanted to see her be a winner at this more than Matt. No one.

Jenny sat with Matt in the dining room of Gringo Bill's the next morning. It was 6:00 a.m. Rosemary, the cook, had brought out their bacon and cheese omelettes, sourdough toast and coffee. Today Jenny was better dressed for the climate, in a white long-sleeved blouse with the cuffs rolled up to her elbows, a sensible set of khaki cotton slacks and her hiking boots. She wore a pair of gold-and-pearl earrings in her dainty earlobes and her hair was tamed into a semblance of order despite the humidity. Outside, the sunlight was nowhere to be seen. Instead, white, wispy clouds crawled in slow, continuous motion around the black lava mountain of Machu Picchu.

As he dug into his omelette, Matt asked, "Did you sleep well last night?"

Coloring, Jenny slathered strawberry jam on her toast. "Okay, I guess. Why?" Matt looked so handsome in his dark green cotton, short-sleeved shirt, his tan chinos and brown hiking boots. She had a tough time not staring and getting lost in his warm gray eyes.

"You were pretty restless last night."

"I was?" She gave him a pained look. "Oh, no…don't tell me I kept you awake?"

He heard the consternation in her whisper. Shaking his head, he smiled slightly. "I woke up once, was all. I went right back to sleep, though." He examined her face from across the small wooden table where they sat. Around them were many other tourists and hikers getting ready to take the bus up to the Incan ruins built atop Machu Picchu.

Touching her cheek, Jenny muttered, "I'm really sorry, Matt. I know how tired you were."

Reaching out, he caught her hand, telling himself as he made intimate contact with her that they should act like a married couple in public to keep their cover intact. Squeezing her fingers, he said, "Hey, I'm more concerned about you. You've got a few shadows under your eyes this morning."

Absorbing his warm, strong touch, she reluctantly released his hand. It was the last thing Jenny wanted to do. Fumbling with the toast, she chewed off an edge of it. Swallowing, she said, "I feel rested. I'm sure I'm sleep deprived sometimes, though."

"You were whimpering in your sleep. Were you having bad dreams?"

Bowing her head, she chewed on her lower lip for a moment. "Oh…that…"

He saw anguish in her fleeting expression. "Your past?" he asked.

Shrugging, Jenny dug nervously into the omelette. She knew she had to eat heartily because of the stress of the interviews to come, even if she had lost her appetite. "Kind of…"

"Want to talk about it? I've got a pretty good set of ears on me if you do."

Just the way he said it broke Jenny's reserve. Ordinarily, she never spoke of her childhood. She wanted to forget about it, but it followed her around like an old and sometimes troublesome friend. Waving her hands nervously, she said, "I'm afraid of the dark…my 'fraidy cat stuff…."

Frowning, Matt said, "There was light coming in around the curtains."

"Not enough for me." Jenny rolled her eyes. "I'm a mess, Matt. I really am. At my apartment in Philipsburg, I have a night-light that I keep on. It helps me sleep better."

"Then," he growled, "I'll find one here in Agua Caliente and we'll put it in our room. For this mission, you need to get your sleep."

She stared across the table at him. Jenny saw the banked anger in his eyes and understood he wasn't angry at her. Grateful, she whispered unsteadily, "You are such a white knight for me…. I know I'm a pain in the butt with all my eccentricities—"

"No, you aren't, darlin'." Matt hesitated. Where had *that* come from? He saw Jenny's eyes widen at the endearment.

Heat tunneled into her face and she instantly fixed her gaze on her plate. She couldn't stand the look Matt gave her. It was a protective, loving look, if she read it correctly. Why would he worry about her? She was nothing to him. She was a nobody. Yet, in her heart, she knew that he did genuinely care, and that rattled her. He'd called her "darlin'."

Scowling, Matt ate several bites of his breakfast, the silence at the table pregnant and tension-filled. Jenny had reacted strongly to his endearment. Because she didn't like him? Considered it sexual harassment? Sometimes he got foot-in-mouth disease. Judging from the redness of her cheeks, she was shocked by it. *Damn.*

Clearing her throat, she said in a low tone, "I remember, when I was growing up, having a stuffed skunk I just loved. I called her Sarah. I don't remember when I got her…only that she'd been with me through all the homes I'd lived in. When I took her to bed with me at night, I felt like she protected me. I started getting scared of the dark when I was sent to another foster home, and my new foster mother didn't want me to have the lamp on in my bedroom. She said I needed to grow up. That a kid my age no longer needed a light or a stuffed toy.''

"How old were you when this happened?"

"Seven...I think." Jenny smiled gamely. "My foster mom was right, of course, but something little and scared deep down inside me just refused to grow up or believe her."

"Is that when you started all this tossing and turning?" He stifled his anger and kept it out of his voice, although he was feeling it sear him inwardly.

"Yes. After my lamp was taken away, and Sarah was gone, I started getting nightmares. You know, dumb stuff like monsters hiding under my bed to get me...hiding in the closet...." Jenny forced herself to eat the toast and jam. The moody look in Matt's eyes made her aware he was upset. "When I got sent to my next foster family, I kept the lamp on in my room, but my foster father would always turn it off and tell me that electricity was expensive, and having a light on all night cost him too much money. By the time I was fifteen, I discovered night-lights, bought one and began to get a reasonable amount of sleep at night." Her smile widened. "I forgot to bring it with me on this trip. My fault."

"I'll see what I can do about finding one for you sometime today, after we get back," Matt muttered, his brow wrinkled. Finishing his food, he wiped his mouth on the paper napkin and glanced over at her. Jenny looked eager to go.

"Ready?" he asked, rising.

"More than ready," she whispered excitedly, leaping to her feet. In rising quickly, she tipped the chair over backward, and it fell with a bang to the wooden floor. The patrons in the dining room all looked up and stopped talking. All eyes centered on her standing over the fallen chair. Jenny grimaced. "I'm such a klutz!" she whispered apologetically as she turned and picked it up.

Matt's heart went out to her. He realized that the stares only exacerbated Jenny's shyness and vulnerability. Coming around the table, he slid his hand into hers and gave her a smile that said everything was going to be all right. How easy it was to pretend he was married to her, he realized in that moment, as hope leaped into her eyes. He felt her shyly return the squeeze of his fingers.

"Let's catch that flight," he murmured.

Jenny gaped as they were taken in a speeding golf cart through a dark, lava tube tunnel from the mining operation side of the mountain to the U.S. Army top secret Black Jaguar base. They had been flown to the area in a civilian helicopter piloted by one of the Black Jaguar personnel, Warrant Officer Jessica Merril. What struck Jenny about this woman pilot was that she, too, had short blond hair—with a bright red streak dyed in it. In Jenny's opinion, it made her look like a wild woman. Merril was outgoing, confident and vibrant. The half-hour flight past the famous Machu Picchu architectural ruins and deep into the jungle was made delightful by the wisecracking army pilot. Jenny didn't know when she'd laughed so much or so long. Indeed, if Jessica mirrored the other female pilots here at this secret base, Jenny was looking forward to meeting these brave and heroic women. Matt had already informed her that at first, the base was made up of only women personnel. But now that was changing and about ten percent of the base was male.

As the golf cart hummed along under the command of the driver, an army sergeant near Jenny's own age, Jenny looked around in awe, especially when they left the tunnel and entered a huge, deep cavern.

"Ohh!" she gasped, turning and gripping Matt's arm. "Look! Omigosh! This is *awesome!*"

"I agree," he murmured, impressed. The huge cavern held not only tent and Quonset hut facilities for the personnel, but a two-story operations building, and a huge landing lip where two Boeing Apache Longbow helicopters and a Blackhawk helo sat. The place was a beehive of activity with people and golf carts coming and going ceaselessly. Matt figured that electricity would be at a premium, and that the base probably ran on those huge generators he'd seen over on the mining side. It was probably that battery-powered golf carts were used to transport people and supplies from one side of the mountain to the other.

Their driver stopped at the small, two-story building with HQ painted in black on its sheet metal siding. Jenny slid out of the golf cart.

"Just go up the stairs, ma'am," the red-haired sergeant said. "Major Stevenson is in room 208. She's awaiting your arrival."

Thanking the sergeant, Jenny hurried up the outside metal grate stairs to the second floor, Matt at her heels. The loud, irritating sound of a bell suddenly clamored through the complex, echoing from the cave walls. Jenny hesitated when she saw four women dressed in black, form-fitting uniforms, helmets in hand, running toward the Apache helicopters, which were being pushed out onto the lip, beyond the cave entrance.

"They've got a mission," Matt told her as he came to a halt by her side and watched the scene unfold. "That bell is telling them to get to their helos and get into the sky. They've probably spotted drug runners on radar and are going to intercept them."

Turning, Jenny looked up at him. Now Matt's face was grim and drawn. She was seeing his warrior side once again. Gazing back at the women climbing into the dual cockpits of the Boeing

Apaches, which were painted a dark green color, she said, "They'll be risking their lives, won't they?"

Nodding, Matt turned and studied her upturned face. "Judging from the report, these pilots risk their lives every time they fly. Look at that hole they've got to fly through...whew, that's tight! One wrong move and they'd crash into the side of that lava wall."

He was right, Jenny realized in mounting alarm. They watched as the cockpit hatches were closed by the crew chiefs and the rotors began to turn. The growl and high-pitched hum of the Apaches' dual engines warming up to take off hurt her sensitive ears. Jenny knew she could never do what these women did. Her admiration for them rose steadily. Turning, she opened the door.

"I think we need to meet Major Stevenson," she told him, glancing down at the gold watch on her right wrist.

He agreed and followed her into the building, down a hallway bustling with women personnel moving to and from the various offices. He and Jenny quickly located Major Stevenson's office on the right side of the corridor.

Jenny halted and knocked on the open door. The woman behind the metal desk looked up.

"You Jenny Wright? From Perseus?"

"Yes, I am. And this is Matt Davis." Jenny moved forward with a confidence she didn't feel, but she had to pretend, for this commanding officer's sake. Maya Stevenson was more than a heroine in her eyes. She was more like a goddess—perhaps Pallas Athena, a wise woman warrior from Greek mythology.

The major's emerald eyes settled squarely on Jenny, but oddly, Jenny no longer felt anxious or worried. Somehow Major Stevenson's look calmed her nervous state. Good leaders had that ability, Jenny was discovering. At home, working for Morgan, she could be in the midst of a high-stress situation but his calm demeanor automatically soothed her, as well.

"Glad you're here, Ms. Wright, Mr. Davis. Have a seat. Let's talk. Coffee?" Major Stevenson said, turning to the coffee machine behind her desk.

Jenny cast a quick look at Matt, who drew out two chairs sitting near the wall and brought them to the center of the small, cramped room. He gave her a look at that said, *Everything's okay, darlin'*. Well, he might not have said "darlin'" but she liked to think he did.

"I'd love some coffee," Jenny said.

"Good. Woman after my own heart," the major murmured as she poured some into a white, chipped mug. "Never trust a person who doesn't drink some java." She cast a look over her shoulder. "Cream? Sugar?"

"Er…no, black, please. Matt? Do you want some?"

He grinned. "I'd better or the major is going to throw me out of here as jaguar bait. Right, Major?"

Jenny heard Major Stevenson chortle as she turned and leaned across the desk to hand her the cup.

"That's right, Mr. Davis. Black?"

"Yes, please."

Jenny saw and felt the instant rapport that Matt established with the major. It was because they were both in the military, which had its own language, slang, and above all, a unique camaraderie that was often tighter than family bonds. Jenny knew she was an outsider to their world. Still, Maya treated her as if she were a part of the group, and for that Jenny was grateful.

After handing Matt his coffee, Major Stevenson sat down. She shoved a stack of files in their direction. "I have seven women who want to volunteer for those missions, Ms. Wright."

"Please, call me Jenny? I'm afraid I don't stand much on formality."

Maya grinned darkly. "Just like your boss, I see. Okay, Jenny. You call me Maya. Fair enough?"

She smiled. "Sure." Leaning forward, Jenny asked, "These are your pilots who want to work with Perseus?"

"Yep." Maya sipped her coffee as she continued

to gauge her from half-closed eyes. "It's your job to figure out which three, Jenny. Morgan Trayhern said you come armed with a psych degree. I like that. You look like you run your life by the seat of your pants. With your intuition, right?"

Shaken by the commanding officer's perception, Jenny straightened and said, "Why, yes...yes, I do."

Nodding brusquely, Maya said, "Good. Don't trust a woman that doesn't run on her gut at all times." She waved her hand toward the files. "You pick 'em, Jenny. And then let's schedule a conference afterward and we'll go over your choices before we post the lucky three names."

"Do you have suggestions? I'd love to be aware of them."

Her grin increased. "Now...I know just enough psychology to shoot myself in the foot with it, Jenny. I feel you need to do this by yourself. You don't need me noodling in with my two cents' worth. You know the mission. You know what it requires. Any one of my pilots would do. But you and Morgan have set up certain protocols. You know the people my women have to interface with, and so it comes down to personalities, doesn't it? Who will get along with whom? And I'm out of that circle. So after you've interviewed my pilots, we'll meet and talk, okay?"

Jenny nodded and sipped her coffee. She saw a

sergeant come in and hand Maya several sheets of faxed papers. Maya thanked her, looked at them and sighed.

"Duty calls." She stood up. "Sergeant Joann Prater will show you to the room you'll use to conduct your interviews in, Jenny. If you need anything, she's your contact. Okay?"

The sergeant, a woman with short, red hair and blue pale eyes, came forward and smiled. "Let me show you to the room, Ms. Wright?"

Jenny quickly got up, balanced her coffee cup and picked up her briefcase, while Matt came forward and scooped up the personnel files. "Thanks, Maya. We hope to have this done in two or three days," Jenny murmured.

Nodding, Maya said, "That's fine. See you later."

Even as Jenny turned, she saw Maya pick up the phone with a dark and harried expression. The faxes must have been upsetting. As she and Matt followed Sergeant Prater down the highly waxed hall to a room near the end on the left, Jenny began to realize the pressure that all these women worked under continuously. Could she work with that kind of stress? No way.

The room was they entered was tiny and spare. There was a green metal desk in the middle, a small window with venetian blinds over it, and several green metal chairs. And that was all. Matt placed the files on the desk and stood back while Jenny put her coffee cup down on it and settled her heavy briefcase on the floor nearby. The sergeant left. The hum of office machines, the low voices of the staff, the ringing of phones, drifted into their space.

Looking around, Jenny set her hands on her hips. "Home. At least for the next few days."

"It could be a lot worse," Matt observed. "By the way, you made a good impression on the major."

"I did?"

"She treated you like one of her own. That's a good sign."

Lifting the briefcase to the desk, she murmured, "I thought she had. I know military people don't necessarily like civilians."

"My gut tells me she likes you."

"Then I've crossed my first bridge. I know if a CO doesn't like you, you're damned."

Chuckling, Matt moved the chairs around so that they were in front of her desk. "You catch on real fast, darlin'. Real fast." This time, he purposely used the endearment to see what effect it would have on her. Jenny lifted her chin and looked at him, her sky-blue eyes flaring with surprise...and pleasure.

"I'll bet you call every woman darlin'," she accused lightly as she pulled out her laptop and hunted for a place to plug it in. Her heart was beating erratically because the look he gave her was one of interest—and desire.

''No,'' Matt answered slowly as he walked to the door and looked out into the hallway, ''I don't.''

Flustered, Jenny sat down, opened up her laptop and turned it on. Watching Matt lean casually against the doorjamb, his hands in the pockets of his chinos, she felt a little shaky and uncertain about their relationship. Tonight, she had to go back to the hostel and sleep in that bed—with him—again. How would she handle it this time?

Chapter Six

Fatigue lapped at Jenny as she sat down on their bed in the hostel. It was nearly ten o'clock and they'd just finished a quick meal at the India Feliz Restaurant. Matt sat at the small desk, reading the information she had typed in on the three women pilots she'd interviewed extensively today.

Untying her hiking boots, Jenny yearned to lay down and sleep. The day had been horrendously stressful on her, although she'd not let that out to anyone. No, she'd behaved confidently, as if she knew exactly what she was doing. Yawning, she stretched out on the bed, her hands tucked beneath the pillow.

Matt glanced up. He saw Jenny closing her eyes and drawing her knees up toward her body. It was dampish in the room and she was lying on top of the quilt. Getting up, he took the light alpaca blanket and spread it across her diminutive form. As he drew it up to her small shoulders, he saw her smile tiredly.

"Thanks…. I'm bushed. I think I'll take a little nap before I get my shower, Matt…."

Her words were slurring. Leaning down, he followed his desire to touch her. Threading his fingers through her short, blond hair, he whispered, "Go to sleep, darlin'. You've earned it. You did a good job up there today." He saw her lips part and realized that she was already asleep. *Good.* Last night she'd been restless, and Matt was sure she hadn't gotten very much sleep.

Tucking the brown-and-cream-colored blanket around her shoulders, he stood above her and absorbed her soft, peaceful features. What a courageous woman she was, and yet she didn't see it or recognize it within herself. Jenny had conducted the three long, intensive interviews with professionalism and intelligence. He'd seen another side to her today and he was very impressed. During the interviews, she wasn't flighty, restless or talkative. She had her questions and she asked them. And she faithfully typed each pilot's answers into her laptop. At all times, she was cordial but reserved, and kept a professional demeanor. Matt figured the degree in psychology had taught Jenny how to handle herself in such a situation.

Going back to the laptop, Matt continued to look at the answers the pilots had given during the interview. Jenny had asked him to go over the material and create comments or follow-up questions, if needed, because, with his military background, he could deduce much more than she along those lines. Jenny was a team player. Throughout the day, she'd made him feel important and part of each interview. He hadn't been relegated to a corner, to be seen but not heard from. Nope, between each interview, she'd spent at least thirty minutes, sometimes an hour, asking for his opinions, his experience, in order to gauge the prospective volunteers.

Hours later, Matt shut down the laptop and took a shower. It was nearly midnight. As he came out of the bathroom, the steam curling out the door as he opened it, he saw that Jenny continued to sleep peacefully. Maybe because he'd purchased a night light at a local vendor's booth on the way back this evening? It burned brightly and steadily in a wall socket. When he'd taken his shower, he'd turned off all the lights with the exception of the night-light.

As he approached the bed, his heart expanded. Matt felt such tenderness toward Jenny. She slept like the angel she was. He recalled how, on their way down the dirt path from the helicopter landing pad, she'd wanted to go visit Maria and little Daniel, to see how they were. Matt and Jenny had gone to the part of town next to the soccer field, where most of the poor lived in shabby tin shacks, with rocks on the roof to hold them down during thunderstorms or on windy days. Maria was just coming back from the roaring tributary that cut through the small town on its way to the mighty Urubamba. She had a load of wet clothes in her huge basket.

Smiling softly, Matt shook his head as he remembered Jenny's kindness. As tired and hungry as she was, she'd followed Maria to her humble home and helped her hang the laundry on several lines outside the shack or down at the river. And she'd also brought Daniel a piece of chocolate cake they'd been served at the base cafeteria. The little boy's eyes had lit up like Christmas tree lights. It was painfully obvious that Jenny dearly loved children. She'd hugged Daniel, kissed his silky black hair and given him the small gift. Maria's husband, Juan, had thanked them for their generosity.

Crouching down now, Matt placed one hand on the side of the bed near Jenny's drawn-up knees, which were tucked warmly beneath the alpaca coverlet. "You're an incredible person, Jenny Wright," he whispered as he trailed his fingertips across her firm, warm cheek. "What are you? A beautiful fairy? A pretty butterfly? You're more a figment of my imagination than real, aren't you?" Matt spoke softly, not wanting to rouse her from her badly needed sleep. When he grazed her cheek, she moved slightly in response. She was so sensitive. So fragile. And yet, despite her difficult years growing up, she pushed courageously forward.

Matt found himself wanting to help Jenny continue to grow, to evolve out of her imprisoned past. She brought out his natural desire to help others. For so long, Jenny had been alone. Matt had discovered earlier today that the few relationships Jenny had had with men had all been negative. She blamed herself, of course, for the outcome of each. However, she never said anything negative or disparaging about men. From Matt's view, knowing only what she shared with him, the men she'd known had been first-class jerks who didn't have a clue how to appreciate someone like Jenny. They couldn't get beyond her restless flightiness, her talkativeness when she got nervous, or her lack of self-esteem.

"No," he whispered softly, "you don't tame a butterfly, do you, darlin'? You just give her her freedom, and appreciate her for what she is and is not...."

Rising slowly, Matt moved around the end of the bed. He pulled back the covers on his side and eased his bulk down, not wanting to disturb Jenny. Once in bed, he lay with his face toward the wall, because if he didn't, he was going to turn on his side, reach out and gently pull Jenny into the curve of his arm. His heart wanted that more than anything…and yet Matt brutally reminded himself that women were trouble with a capital *T*. His ex-wife had taught him that.

Tomorrow was another day, and he found himself looking forward more than ever to working with Jenny. She was mesmerizing to him; she had so many facets, like a gleaming, brilliant diamond. And he was enjoying discovering the many scintillating and wonderful sides to her. Yes, tomorrow was another day. A delicious day full of possibilities….

Jenny held her breath momentarily when Chief Warrant Officer Akiva Redtail walked into the interview room. She was copper-skinned, with gold, slightly tilted eyes. Though she wore the same black, body-hugging uniform the other pilots did, several things set her apart from the women Jenny had interviewed yesterday. Mostly it was the invisible yet powerful energy that Jenny felt surrounding the nearly six foot tall, big-boned woman pilot. It nearly knocked Jenny over as Akiva Redtail soundlessly entered the room. Akiva's hair, thick and black, hung straight and shining down across her breasts. She wore a bright red headband that brought out her obvious Native American looks. What caught Jenny's attention was a small braid started at the center part and tucked neatly behind her right ear. Around her waist, tucked in her belt, was a very old-looking ax covered with leather, the aged handle knicked and well worn. On her right side, near her pistol, she wore a beaded Indian scabbard with short fringe that held a huge knife.

"Hi, Ms. Wright," Akiva Redtail said, thrusting out her hand across the desk. "I hear you're the woman who's gonna pick the lucky three?"

Jenny couldn't help but smile at this bold, confident pilot. She gripped her hand and shook it warmly. "That's right, but Mr. Davis, my partner here, was in the military, and will be helping me make the final choices. Have a seat? I'll try and make this as fast as possible."

The pilot released Jenny's hand and went over to Matt and shook his. "Yeah, I've got the dirty duty today. Let's hope the cowbell doesn't ring." And she grinned wolfishly as she sat down. Taking a huge wad of bubble gum out of her cheek, she threw it in the wastebasket nearby.

"I chew bubble gum when I'm on duty. Reduces my stress level," she explained as she sat comfortably, one booted leg across the other.

"I'd probably drink," Jenny said wryly. "I admire what you pilots do. It's dangerous work."

"Thanks. It's nice to get a compliment from the outside. Not many know about us, or what we do," the woman agreed good-naturedly. She looked around the spare office. "But it's home and we love it here. We're good at what we do and we know it.'' She flashed a huge smile. ''I like being in trench warfare. It's where the action is, and I was born for action.''

Smiling, Jenny typed in the pilot's name into her laptop. She liked Akiva Redtail immensely. There was such warmth and joviality in her shining golden eyes, which missed nothing. Opening her personnel file, Jenny studied it for a moment and then looked up at her.

''I'm going to hang myself out on a limb here and tell you I'm completely ignorant of Native American people. Could you help me understand where you've come from? Your background? That way, I'll have a better idea of how you might fit into this upcoming mission with Perseus.''

''Absolutely. What do you want to know? I'm an open book,'' Akiva said, and she laughed heartily.

''I hope you don't think I'm insulting you,'' Jenny said, ''but you have a beautiful name. May I call you Akiva? And can you tell me about the name? How you got it? As well as your background.''

Raising her thick, arched brows, Akiva nodded. ''Sure, no problem. I'm half Charicauha Apache and half Santee Lakota. On my mother's side, the Apache side, my great-great-grandmother rode with Geronimo. She was one of his women warriors.''

"A woman warrior?" Jenny gasped. "Really? I didn't know Apaches allowed women to fight."

Chuckling indulgently, Akiva gave her a wry look. "My dear, Apaches are a matriarchal society. If a woman has what it takes to be a warrior, then she becomes one. Warrior blood runs in my veins. And my great-great-grandmother rode for years with Geronimo, until they were suckered into a trap by the U.S. Army and she was shot in the back, paralyzed, and eventually died, months afterward. She was his greatest warrior and he relied heavily on her. After that attack, Geronimo fled back to Mexico."

Akiva pointed to the ax and the knife in her belt. "See these weapons? They belonged to my great-great-grandmother. She used them, too. And they've been passed down through our family. My mother gave them to me when I entered the U.S. Army. Just before I joined, I became an Apache warrior. It involves a long, tough endurance test." She pointed to the braid on her head. "See this? This is what is known as the third braid of the warrior. Only an Apache man or woman can wear it, after they've passed many, many grueling, life-and-death tests to earn it. I earned my third braid at age seventeen."

"Wow!" Jenny whispered, caught up in Akiva's story. "What a wonderful family background. Women warriors...and look at you now."

"Yeah, instead of a horse, I ride a Boeing Apache

Longbow around instead. Extreme, dude, isn't it?''
She chuckled. ''But I love it. I just have a horse of
a different color, is all. I'm still doing what I do
best, which is to fight for right and light.''

''And your name? Does it mean something?''

''Native American names always mean something, Ms. Wright. Akiva is from my Apache side.
When we do ceremony, we create a kiva, or a place
where the sacred ceremony can be held. My grandmother and mother were both medicine women.
They had jaguar medicine. You know, back in their
day, jaguars roamed the Southwest freely. Each of
my relations confronted and traded spirits with their
jaguars.'' Akiva smiled lethally. ''And I got 'em
now, myself. Can you feel them around me?''

Jenny sat back, amazed. ''Jaguar medicine?''

''Sure. My grandmother gave me her jaguar spirit
guide when she died. My mother recently passed
over and gave me hers. Now I have two, and believe
me, I use 'em all the time in my business. Their
eyes and ears alert me to Russian Kamov helicopters
that are out there lurkin' around and wanting to
shoot us out of the sky. They warn me. Sorta like a
strong gut intuition, you know?''

Fascinated, Jenny absorbed Akiva's intensity and
fell captive to her narrowed golden eyes. She could
easily fantasize that Akiva was more jaguar than
woman, and Jenny almost swore for a fleeting moment that she saw the face of a jaguar superimposed

over Akiva's own features. Blinking, Jenny laughed awkwardly and chided herself for her overactive imagination. "There's no doubt, I sure feel power around you. Now I know why."

Nodding as if pleased with herself, Akiva said, "Extreme. That's me. If you're looking for someone to carry out an impossible mission, then you've got to think of me first."

"No doubt," Jenny said. "If Akiva comes from your Apache side of the family, is your last name, Redtail, from your Lakota side?"

She crossed her legs and leaned forward. "Yes, it is. My father's family are Santee Lakota and live in Nebraska. Redtail is his family name. They took the name when the U.S. Army made them come up with a first and last name. The red-tailed hawk is our family totem." She grinned and pointed to her eyes. "I have hawk eyes, too. I can see things a lot of other pilots can't. I don't miss anything."

"And so you have hawk medicine, as well." Jenny guessed.

"You got it." Akiva smiled hugely. "I think Major Stevenson ought to keep you around, Ms. Wright. You got the right stuff. You're fast on your feet and you fit right in with us rebels with a cause."

Jenny felt heat flood her face at the pilot's sincere praise. The look in Akiva's eyes reminded her of a hawk measuring its competitors. It was clear the pilot desperately wanted this mission. And at the same time, Akiva had the good grace to admire Jenny herself, for what she brought to the interview. Feeling a flood of confidence flowing into her at Akiva's words, she glanced to her right to look at Matt, to see his expression. He was gauging Akiva as he had all the others—with his poker face intact.

Jenny looked back at the pilot. "Tell me why you'd want this mission, Akiva?"

Getting up, she smoothed out her uniform. "I'm good at what I do. I understand there're three positions open. I want to be considered *only* for the undercover assignment. I don't care about the one on the border, and training those guys how to fly at night and pick up drug planes comin' to the U.S." She waved her hand and shook her head. "I want the undercover assignment. I speak five languages besides English. Spanish comes easy to me." She pointed to her skin and grinned. "I *look* Mexican, don't you think? I pass for a South American all the time. I understand that mission will be based in Mexico, although I know little else about it. I feel that, with my keen intuition and my ability to think on my feet, I could successfully fulfill that mission's requirements."

"And going undercover doesn't scare you?"

Shrugging dramatically, Akiva said, "I'm scared all the time, Ms. Wright. I live scared. The difference between me and most people is that I can *think through* my fear and know what to do to get the job done. That is what separates me from most others.''

Admiring her strength, her beauty and confidence, Jenny said, ''You make good points, Akiva.''

''I always do.''

Jenny smiled. How she wished she could have just a cup of Akiva's confidence, which radiated from her like rays of sunlight! Not only was Akiva empowered as a woman who fully embraced who and what she was, she thrived on her power, as well. Jenny couldn't fault her for having a healthy ego. Under the circumstances, with the danger these women faced daily, one needed a strong ego and a boatload of confidence, to boot. Akiva was honest about herself and her skills, but she could also reach out and praise others.

''Do you prefer to work alone or with a partner?''

Akiva moved around the room, her hands on her hips as she hung her head in thought. Walking slowly in a circle, she came to a halt in front of the desk and looked at Jenny.

''It would depend upon the circumstance. As a woman, I'm naturally inclined toward teamwork. But there's a side of me that is perfectly happy running the gauntlet alone, too. Maybe it's my Apache blood.'' And she flashed her a white, even smile of pride. ''I'm easy either way, Ms. Wright.''

''What if the mission required you to work on

your own? You wouldn't have a partner. No backup. No help if things turned bad.''

Akiva lifted her strong chin and looked around. ''Sounds like my life around here.'' She chuckled derisively, then became serious. ''We're always on the slats because we can't ID the Russian Kamov attack helicopter radar signature on our equipment. If things turn bad out there, then it's them against us. There's no U.S. Cavalry arriving. Just Perseus and Morgan Trayhern.'' She smiled thinly. ''Isn't this a hoot? Two generations later, I'm a part of the very U.S. Army that chased down and killed my great-great grandmother. How's that for karma?''

''It is,'' Jenny agreed, quickly typing in her answer. ''So, it wouldn't bother you to live alone, on alert every day in a remote site in the jungle, with no help at all?''

''No.'' Akiva's eyes narrowed to slits. ''I have my own backup from another world, Ms. Wright. I know you Anglos in North America don't believe in spirit guides, but we Indians do. And they are just as real as you and I. You don't have to believe that. But I do. I've had it proved to me time and again that my spirit guides not only help me, but guide me, and have more than once saved my butt from a sling.'' She punched the air with her finger. ''I have my spirit jaguars—two extra sets of eyes, ears, noses—to keep me alive and fighting.''

The energy swirled and shifted dramatically

around the room. Jenny felt it. So, obviously, did Matt. He moved uncomfortably, but said nothing. Akiva stood there, hands on her hips, defiant, self-assured, that unseen power palpable. Jenny felt as if a lightning bolt had struck the desk between them. She felt addled and confused in the wake of it.

"I believe you," she told Akiva, faithfully typing in her answer.

Just then, the alarm bell rang. Jenny jerked her head up at the sound. She saw Akiva's face go hard and her eyes narrow to predatory slits. In one smooth, unbroken motion, she whirled around, her black hair a swirling cape around her shoulders as she sped out the door and down the hall.

"Whew!" Jenny said as she stood up. "She is *something else,* Matt!"

Rising, he moved to the door and watched the flurry of action as the bell continued to ring throughout the complex. Once a drug plane or helicopter had been spotted by the base radar operator, the bell was rung and the two Apaches and supporting Blackhawk lifted off in pursuit soon after. Such a response entailed a lot of fast action on the part of the ground team, as well as the pilots.

Turning, Matt saw that Jenny's eyes were huge with excitement. He smiled a little and leaned against the door. "You almost look like you want to run out there with Akiva and jump in that Apache and take off with her."

"Don't I wish!" Jenny touched her cheek, her voice filled with awe. "I wish...oh, how I wish I possessed that kind of raw courage and confidence. She is just so incredibly strong and self-assured about herself and what she can do."

"Don't be so quick to condemn yourself," Matt warned her darkly as he pushed away from the door and ambled toward the desk. "Not everyone needs to be a warrior on the front lines like these women are. The support group behind them is equally important. Without them, those helos wouldn't be serviced, fueled up—they wouldn't go anywhere. And the office people are handling the traffic, the phone calls, the in-house operation that coordinates everything from bombs to bullets that those big rigs are outfitted with."

Nodding, Jenny said, "You're right." She realized he was referring to behind-the-scene people like her—who helped Morgan keep Perseus running effectively. The look in Matt's eyes was one of admiration for what she and others like her did, and it made her heart soar. Shutting off the laptop, Jenny sat back down. "We haven't even had a chance to talk about last night."

He grinned and sat on the edge of the desk. "Oh? You mean your falling asleep and not taking a shower before you hit the hay?"

Wrinkling her nose, she said, "Yes."

"I didn't notice any odor, if that's what you're gnashing your worrywart teeth over."

She laughed at his gentle teasing. "You're reading my mind!"

"Well, when every expression flits across that beautiful face of yours, it's kinda hard not to know what you're thinking or feeling."

A delicious warmth infused her heart, and Jenny felt euphoric as he gave her that special look. She could drown, literally, in Matt's gray eyes.

"Beautiful? Me? Hardly. Now, if you want beautiful, look at Akiva. She's gorgeous! She's so primal and wild-looking, a very earthy, sensual woman."

"That's one kind of beauty," Matt agreed, crossing his arms and watching Jenny fiddle with her paper and pencils. He saw the look in her blue eyes and recognized how much she really *wanted* to believe he thought she was truly beautiful. She *was* beautiful. All he had to do was convince her of it. "Your beauty, on the other hand, is not so dramatic, but it's just as moving to a man, believe me."

"Oh?" Jenny met and held his smoldering look. Her skin prickled deliciously as his gaze slid to her mouth, lingered there and then moved down across the rest of her body. She had never felt this way about a man before—as if his gaze was a physical touch grazing her heightened, sensitive flesh. It was a wonderful feeling. One that made her ache to kiss him, to slide her hands in a ranging, exploratory motion across his powerful, darkly haired chest. Gulping unsteadily at her wild thoughts, she felt it must be Akiva's primal presence that was making her feel like a wild woman!

"Your beauty is quiet, warm sunlight to a man's starving, cold soul," Matt told her quietly. "Your warmth, your spontaneity and generosity of heart would melt the hardest of hearts, darlin'." He wanted to add, *And you've melted my heart to the point to where all I can do is think about touching you, kissing those petal-soft lips of yours, making you mine in every possible way.... want to feel you breathe. I want to breathe with you and flow into your welcoming body and feel your arms wrap around me and heal my wounds. Heal me....* But he didn't. He said nothing as he absorbed her gentle blue gaze, which glinted with gold in the aftermath of his warm praise of her.

Matt wondered how he was going to maintain his distance from her in bed each night. Because of the pilots' schedules, and their sporadic and unexpected flight missions due to drug trafficking, the interviews were going to take much longer than first anticipated. That meant more nights with her. How in the hell was he going to keep his hands off her?

Chapter Seven

"I can't sleep," Jenny sighed as she twisted to look to her right. Matt lay with his hands behind his head. In the dull light that filtered in through the window and the glow of the night-light, she could see his rugged profile and the set of his mouth. It was nearly midnight, according to the luminous dials on her watch.

"Me neither," he rumbled.

"I keep running those interviews over in my mind. Darn, the pilots we've interviewed so far are *all* up to handling the missions that Mike Houston designed for Perseus."

"Especially Akiva. She's good merc material. I

know Morgan would love to steal her away from here and offer her a job at Perseus.''

''Ohh,'' Jenny whispered in an admiring tone, ''she is so unique! You're right—Morgan would fall all over himself trying to get her to join us. I love her rock solid confidence. It's so nice to see that in a woman. I mean, all the women pilots have it, but she's *really* got it.''

One corner of Matt's mouth lifted. ''You have it, too, you know.''

She turned onto her side and allowed herself the complete luxury of staring at him in the gray light of their room. Jenny had come to look forward to these nights shared with Matt. She was sleeping well now. Maybe it was the night-light…or maybe it was Matt, who gave her such a sense of safety.

Jenny saw him slant her an amused look. ''I feel more confident since coming here,'' she admitted. ''I think it's because of you, as well as how the women pilots treat me. They respect me.''

Moving onto his side, Matt propped himself up on one elbow. It took everything not to reach out and graze Jenny's ruffled hair or slide his aching fingertips across the smooth slope of her cheek. As his gaze dropped to her parted lips, he groaned inwardly. What would she feel like beneath his mouth? How would she taste? Tearing his mind from below his waist, he murmured, ''What you don't realize is a lot of people respect you. You're just the last to see it.'' He saw her give him a funny, sad smile.

''Maybe…'' With her fingertip, Jenny drew an invisible pattern on the sheet, between them. Her heart was starting to pound again, and she knew why. She wanted to reach out and touch Matt's hard, dark jaw. Even though he shaved each morning, by this time of night his beard darkened his face once more, giving him a very dangerous, dark look that thrilled her.

''What about you, Matt? You always want to know about me. You never speak about yourself…your past…or what brought you to this point in your life.''

''Uh-oh,'' he teased, ''here comes twenty questions.''

Giggling, Jenny held his warm gaze and felt a luscious sheet of heat flow downward, to pool languorously in her lower body, where a throbbing ache was centered. ''I know you're a merc, and I know you value secrets. But couldn't you share just a little bit about yourself with me? After all, I was an open book to you. I trusted you enough to tell you about my embarrassing life, thus far.''

To hell with it. He reached out and cupped Jenny's chin and held her widening blue gaze. ''Listen to me, darlin'. You have nothing to be ashamed of about your past or your childhood. You had it rough. And you've survived. I'm really proud of you, Jenny. You've come a long way. You were handed nothing but rags and yet you made a rainbow quilt with them.''

His fingers were gentle as they curved against her cheek and jaw. Closing her eyes, she trembled as she absorbed his tentative touch. When he withdrew his fingers, she slowly opened her eyes. A feeling of dizziness, of craving him, of wanting more than she deserved, gnawed through her heart and body.

''A rainbow quilt,'' she said quietly. ''Is that how you see my life?'' She watched his smile form; it was a smile of a wolf hunting its chosen prey. Yet it didn't make her feel uncomfortable. Rather, she felt wanted and desired. Jenny had never had a man look at her quite the way Matt did. Was she reading the signals wrong? If he really desired her, why didn't he kiss her? Why didn't he speak of how he felt about her? Or was he just into having a one-night stand? Jenny wouldn't go for that…ever. She'd made mistakes with men before, but she'd learned from each of them. There had to be a lot more than raw sex to a relationship. There had to be a genuine enjoyment, a friendship, between two people, too. The thought flitted through her head that she wasn't brave enough to pursue a relationship with Matt. In her mind's eye, she imagined he would be drawn to a woman from the military who had the same kind of background, plus that similar raw courage that Jenny certainly didn't possess. A little saddened over that thought, she absorbed his growing smile.

"You're a rainbow, all right," Matt said as he forced his hand to rest between them on the sheet. The ache in his lower body was intensifying—rapidly. He wanted to take her. To drown in her soft blue eyes, worship those petal-shaped lips and feel her womanly arms around him, holding him as only a woman could do.

"That's nice," Jenny said with a sigh. "Do you know how I see you?"

Matt saw the unsureness come into her expression as she boldly blurted her questions. Jenny tucked her lower lip between her teeth, a sign that she was nervous about putting out a tentative feeler in his direction. "How do you see me?" In order to ease her tension, he teased, "Like a clam? Armored up? Like a wall?"

Laughing breathily, she said, "No, not at all! I see you..." she lifted her eyes toward the darkness of the ceiling momentarily "...as a wonderful knight in shining armor."

Groaning, Matt said, "Jenny, I'm not. Just ask my ex-wife. I might have been the Don Quixote type of knight in her eyes, but that's about it." He chuckled derisively.

Jenny had been waiting for him to open up to her, and she knew this was her chance to gently delve into his past. "What was she like—your ex-wife?"

Matt rolled his eyes. "Marilyn is a red-haired attorney. A criminal trial attorney. A shark of the first order."

"You must have seen something in her you loved?"

With a grimace, Matt muttered, "Yeah, I did. I liked her passion, her fire, her belief in battling for the underdogs of life and helping people who couldn't normally afford a lawyer like her. She was a top gun at a big law firm, and what I liked about her was that she cared for the little people of the world. Always. Marilyn never looked down on them." Rubbing his face to wipe away the tiredness that was lapping at him, Matt added, "I make her out to be a demon, but she's not, really. She just raked me over the coals when we got divorced, and I'm still smarting from it."

"I've seen some divorces turn awfully nasty," Jenny agreed glumly.

"Ours was. It didn't have to be, but we were both hardheaded and stubborn. Neither of us would give in to the other. I ended up on the short end of the stick, and I guess, being honest about it, I'm a sore loser. I need to let it and her go."

"Did you have any children?" Jenny asked. She saw the anguish and pain in Matt's darkening eyes.

"No, thank God we didn't."

"Did you want any?"

"Yes, but we decided we'd wait until we were in

our mid-thirties. Marilyn had her career, and I was shifting from the U.S. Navy to Perseus at the time. We didn't feel it would be fair to bring a child into a home where both parents were fighting for new, higher-paying career slots.''

''That's great that you thought of those things. A child could suffer under that kind of situation.'' Jenny liked the idea that Matt was sensitive to what it would take to raise a child.

''Yeah, you would be especially sensitive to that issue, since you were traded around from one foster family to another,'' he replied. ''I know you like kids. Daniel thinks you're his second mother,'' he chuckled. Even tonight, after they'd been flown back to Agua Caliente, Jenny had walked to the river, where Maria was washing the clothes of her many clients. The older woman was methodically pounding the wet garments with a large, smooth stone while Daniel played nearby in a pool that had been created by the townspeople for small children. No one would dare to try and swim, much less cross, the wild hundred-foot-wide tributary, which poured like a rabid, frothing dog into the Urubamba downstream.

Jenny had once again brought the child the dessert she'd gotten at the Black Jaguar Base mess, and Daniel had been thrilled. And she had bought Maria several worn, dark green wool blankets that Major Stevenson had said she could distribute to the poor.

Maria had stood there, blankets in hand, with tears of gratitude in her eyes. Little Daniel had toddled up, his hands covered with chocolate frosting after having eaten the cake, and gripped Jenny's slacks. She hadn't cared that the little boy was messy, and had picked him up, kissed him on the cheek and hugged him lovingly.

"Someday," Jenny whispered now, giving Matt a dreamy smile, "I want children."

"How many?"

"Two, I think. Two is plenty. It takes so much money to raise them, nowadays. I'd like to give them the opportunities I never had. To make their lives a little easier, so that they can follow their dreams, whatever they may be."

"You'll be one hell of a mother," Matt rasped, meaning every word. He itched to reach out and touch her. Matt saw the languid look in her darkening eyes as she stared across those scant inches at him. Her lips parted.

Taking a deep breath, he closed his eyes. "I think I'd better tell you that you're in danger, Jenny."

Her eyes widened enormously. "What?" Instantly, she sat up. The sheet slid and pooled around her hips.

He stared up at her. The white cotton nightgown she wore was simple, yet feminine, with lace around the scoop neck. She had clasped her hands against her breasts, her expression truly one of concern.

"Calm down," he told her heavily, and he reached out and slid his hand along her arm. Her skin was soft and warm. Inviting.

"What's the danger?" She began to look around the room. "Spies?"

"No…me."

Snapping her head to the right, Jenny stared down at him. He reminded her of a cougar lazily stretched out on a boulder. The powerful feelings around him, and what she saw in his eyes, helped her make the connection. "Oh…" Gulping, she said, "I think we'd better talk."

Nodding, Matt gave her a grim look. Jenny was like a startled, beautiful deer in that moment. The look in her eyes was one of shock and disbelief. Why? Didn't she know how beautiful she was? How precious to him? How achingly desirable?

"I'm having one hell of a time keeping my hands off you, if you want the truth," he growled. "I don't know what's happened, Jenny. You have a way of getting under a man's armor. Reaching out and touching his heart. At least, that's how I feel about it. I don't know when or how it happened, but it has. And I'm looking at the fact that we're sharing the same bed and that I want to share a lot more than just the space on it with you."

Her breath jammed in her throat. Staring at him, Jenny opened her mouth in amazement. "Y-you like me?"

Giving her a lazy, amused look, Matt said, "Like? That's an understatement, Jenny. I *want* you. In every conceivable way. But I'm not sure about you…about how you feel toward me. There's just something magical about you. You're a butterfly, you know? Beautiful. Distant. And I feel like if I reach out to drag you into my arms and kiss you until we melt together, that I might scare you—destroy you—in the process. In some ways, I see you as being so fragile…." His brows dipped and he stared down at his darkly haired hand, resting on the sheet between them. "This has got to be mutual or it isn't going anywhere. And I don't know where it might lead. I don't have a damned clue. All I know is that I want you. I like listening to you talk. I like sharing life stories with you. You make me laugh— did you know that? I wake up in the morning looking forward to the day with you, and I haven't felt that way in a long, long time. I enjoy your company. I like seeing the world through your idealistic eyes, because the way I look at life, it's a helluva lot uglier. You make me feel clean inside, Jenny…I don't know how else to explain it. I know I'm not very good with words and all…."

Jenny sat very still. His words cascaded across her like warm, unexpected sunlight. "I—it's so hard to believe what I'm hearing, Matt. I mean…" She cleared her throat, her voice wobbling. "I never thought you'd be interested in someone like *me*. I thought you'd be more interested in one of those women pilots we're interviewing. A strong, confident woman. Not someone who shrieks over seeing a spider.''

He gave her a cutting smile. ''I see you as confident. I see your self-assurance blooming. And so what if you screech over a spider? I'm afraid of things, too. We all are.''

Placing her hands on her reddening cheeks, Jenny whispered rawly, ''I didn't know, Matt. I didn't think I was... I didn't think that you...'' She closed her eyes. Her stomach turned, not from fright or fear, but from a wild desire that coursed through her in that moment. Heart fluttering, all she could do was sit there and feel her way through Matt's unexpected admittance.

''Listen, this is *my* problem, Jenny. I just wanted to warn you, so that if some night I accidentally, in my sleep, turn over and pull you into my arms, you won't be shocked. Just give me an elbow in the chest and I'll wake up and let go of you. Okay?''

She could feel her heart pounding beneath her palms, which were pressed to the center of her chest. Looking over at him, Jenny saw how unhappy he appeared. ''This is so shocking, Matt. I never thought you'd have the *least* interest in me!''

''No man in his right mind wouldn't be interested in you, Jenny.'' He saw pain reflected in her eyes.

As she placed her hand on the sheet between them, Matt put his hand over hers in a protective gesture.

"Well, that's not been my experience. They haven't exactly been beating down my door, Matt. I've had two relationships and they were disasters…at least for me." She hung her head and felt his hand move gently across hers in a soothing motion. It gave her the courage to go on. "You might as well know the rest of my life story. I fell hard for a guy name Mark, in college, when I was working toward my degree. I was a lot worse than I am now." She gave Matt a wry look and a weak laugh to try and make a joke of it. But her attempt failed.

"What do you mean?"

"I'm ADD, remember? Ants in my pants. Can't sit still. Constant motion. Restless. Talkative. I warned Mark about my…lacking, and how I was. He didn't seem to care, but as our relationship developed, it did bother him. The night-light bothered him. And he didn't want to talk. Oh, I know men in general aren't good at communicating…but he said I never shut up. That hurt."

"Sure it would." Matt wanted to find Mark and rearrange his immature face for him. "Go on…"

Grimacing, Jenny pulled her hand from beneath his and drew up her knees. She wrapped her arms around them and rested her chin on top. Her voice was hesitant and riddled with confusion. "I just couldn't be what Mark wanted, so I broke up with him.''

"That was a healthy thing to do. If he couldn't accept you as you are, then you weren't going to have many positive things left between you."

"Right. Well, that burned me but good, and I swore off men for a long time. I just kept my nose to the grindstone for a couple of years. In my senior year, I met Bobby. Actually, he chased me for months before I gave in and had a date with him. Oh! This is so embarrassing to tell you, Matt...." She shut her eyes tightly for a moment.

Sitting up, Matt leaned against the headboard and rearranged the sheet around his waist. The agony in Jenny's voice tore at him. Lifting his hand, he moved it lightly across her tense, drawn-up shoulders. "Was he just chasing you to get you in bed? A one-night stand?" he guessed.

Nodding, Jenny turned and looked at Matt, relishing the feel of his hand as it moved slowly across her shoulders. "Yes. I fell for it. Me. At twenty-two, I fell for it. I knew better. I guess I was hoping that Mark was wrong. He said no one would want someone like me in their life. I'd drive them crazy." Matt's features darkened and a flash of anger sparked to life in his narrowing gray eyes. His hand left her shoulders. Inwardly, Jenny cried out for his continued touch.

"So I'm gun-shy. That's why I find it hard to

believe you'd be interested in me. You're a hero, Matt. A genuine hero, with ribbons and medals to prove it. You're a true warrior. And yet you're so kind and sensitive underneath that armor you wear.''

''And you think that what I just shared with you means I want a one-night stand with you, right?''

Jenny avoided his sharpening gaze. His mouth stretched into a thin line. Hurting, she barely got out the whispered word, ''Yes...''

''Because you don't think you're worth a long-term relationship, right?''

Cringing inwardly, she nodded. ''Who wants a coward in their life, Matt?

''Listen to me,'' he said roughly as he settled his hands over her shoulders and turned her toward him, her knees pressing against his hip. Her eyes widened. ''How about deleting 'coward' and inserting 'survivor' instead?'' Matt tightened his fingers around her small shoulders and leaned down until his face was inches from hers. His emotions took hold of him and his voice lowered to a vibrating growl. ''You have survived more adversity from birth onward than most people are ever given. You didn't become a drug addict like your mother, and you could have. You have ADD, but you've learned how to live your life and get along in the world with it, regardless. And you've got a degree in psychology, which clearly shows your discipline, endurance and drive. In my eyes, Jenny, you're a heroine of the first order.'' He gave her a small shake to emphasize the fiery words, which tore out of him in a blaze of frustration, anger and desire. He wanted so badly for her to know how wonderful a human being she really was, that others didn't see her as she saw herself. ''You want to know what *real* courage is? It's living life, day in and day out, the best you can, darlin'. It's about trying to be a decent human being even if you're tired, you're feeling rotten or life has been kicking the hell out of you. It's about struggling to always treat others with respect, with kindness and as your equal.''

Matt eased his grip on Jenny as he drowned in her tear-filled eyes. ''You *are* those things, Jenny! You're a heroine in my eyes and my heart. You're a true survivor—*not* a coward. I want you to take what I'm saying to heart. Please. If I have any influence at all on you, let my honesty replace how you see yourself, okay?''

Hot tears squeezed from her eyes. ''Oh, Matt…'' She lifted her hands and placed them on his broad, powerful shoulders.

Unable to bear seeing her cry, he whispered raggedly, ''I want to hold you, Jenny. Please? I want to give you a safe place. I promise, no funny stuff. Just let me hold you for a little while? I can't stand to see a woman or kid cry. It just tears the hell out of me…''

She crawled into Matt's opening arms. How wonderful it felt, Jenny decided, as he leaned back against the headboard and drew her deeply into his strong embrace. Resting her cheek against his shoulder, his jaw against her hair, she closed her eyes and shyly slid her arms around his torso. Just feeling his hand move protectively across the back of her nightgown, then up to sift gently through her hair, brought more tears to her tightly shut eyes.

"I...never knew.... I just never knew...." she sobbed.

Gruffly, he whispered against her silky hair, "What? That you're a good person, Jenny? That you're courageous already, even if you're the last to realize it? Why do you think Major Stevenson and those pilots respect you? Not one made fun of you. They *admire* you, darlin'. You just don't see it." Breathing out savagely, Matt continued to hold her soft form against his harder one. Sweet mercy, how he wanted to kiss her. But he couldn't...he didn't dare make that move unless Jenny made it first. He swore he would not take advantage of her like Mark and that other jerk had. Right now, as she wept unashamedly in his arms, her small body trembling with each sob, he wanted to give her a safe harbor from the rugged life she'd endured alone thus far.

Grinding his teeth with anger, Matt glared up into the grayness of the quiet room. If he had anything to do with it, Jenny's days of being alone, feeling as if she were a loser and a coward, were over. Matt wasn't exactly sure how he would make that happen, only that his heart told him to do it. Jenny was worthy of love. She was one of the most outwardly giving, loving people he'd ever run across. Matt knew, without a doubt, that he wasn't perfect. Far from it. But he wasn't like the men of her past, either. He valued a long-term relationship. Was there hope for them? Would she consider him more than just a working partner on this mission?

Matt was scared. As he closed his eyes, sighed raggedly and simply absorbed the warmth and fluid feminine length of Jenny in his arms, he was more scared than he could ever recall being. And he was unsure of what else to say. Or do. Or how far to go with her. What it all boiled down to was that Jenny had to make the next move. He had to wait and be patient. To let the shock and trauma and beauty of tonight's honest baring of their souls settle within her heart and mind. That would take time.

Did they have it? How many days were left here? Matt knew that as soon as they got back to Perseus HQ, he had another mission waiting for him, and he'd be gone for another three months. Dammit, anyway. Life was not fair.

Chapter Eight

It took everything Jenny had the next morning after they arrived at Black Jaguar Base, to set aside thoughts of the incredible tenderness and care that Matt had shared with her earlier. Her body still sang from the way he'd held her, as if she were a priceless, delicate and beautiful vase that would surely shatter if he clasped her too tightly in his strong, warm arms. Oh, she wouldn't break, Jenny knew. What Matt didn't realize was that she had a ribbon as strong as steel winding through her.

Matt was sitting to one side in their small cubicle of an office, sipping his hot coffee, when the first interviewee of the day came to the door. A woman with eyes to match the sable color of her shoulder-length hair came and knocked lightly on the opened door. She was about five foot six inches tall, firmly muscled and with a narrow face. Although she wore no rank identification on her black uniform, Matt knew it was Captain Sarah Klein, the XO—executive officer—of the base. She was Major Stevenson's right hand, and a big part of why the base ran so successfully. He watched covertly as Jenny stood and offered her hand to the XO.

"Hi, Captain Klein," Jenny said. "Come in, please. I know you're busier than a one-armed paper hanger around here. Have a seat and we'll get this interview done as fast as possible so you can get back to work."

"Thanks, and call me Dallas, will you? It's what everyone calls me." She turned and nodded in Matt's direction. "Good morning, Mr. Davis."

Impeccable manners. Conservative and diplomatic. Matt nodded and kept the analysis to himself. "Good morning, Dallas. You had your java yet?" He pointed to the coffee machine located on the sideboard near Jenny's desk.

Laughing huskily, Dallas said, "Oh, yes. My day started at 0400 when one of our maintenance crews had an unexpected mechanical problem with our Blackhawk. I'm running full bore on my wire-walking coffee routine, thanks. One more cup and you'll have to scrape me off the ceiling,'' she added with a chuckle.

Jenny grinned. She liked Dallas immediately. The XO position required a lot of hard behind-the-scenes work, judging from what Matt had told her earlier on their flight from Agua Caliente to the base. The commanding officer created the orders and the XO catalyzed them and made things happen. It was the hardest job in a squadron, from what Matt had told her. And looking at Dallas, who relaxed, one leg across the other, her long, spare hands in her lap, she could see the care-worn quality to her face, the tiredness lurking beneath her sparkling sable eyes.

Still, there was a softness at the corners of the pilot's mouth, and Jenny found herself liking the woman without really even knowing why. Dallas inspired her simply with her quiet, easygoing, steady presence. Maybe it was the woman's face, which was narrow and oval, with a strong chin, aquiline nose and large, liquid, deerlike eyes, that bestowed a sense of calm around Dallas and made Jenny feel at ease.

Quickly opening up her personnel file, Jenny asked, ''Why do you want to volunteer for the border trading mission, Dallas? Aren't you busy enough around here?''

A smile lurked on her well-shaped mouth. Opening her hands, she said, ''Even an XO needs a change of pace every once in a while. I asked

Maya—Major Stevenson—what she thought of me thinking about volunteering for such an assignment because of the heavy responsibilities and duties I have around her. I asked her if she could get along without me for three months.''

''And could she?''

Dallas shrugged. ''She said she could. Maya lies well.'' She chuckled indulgently. ''But she also knows I've been XO for three years now, and I need a mental health break from all this…'' she waved her hand toward the door ''…crazy activity.''

''So, you see this mission up on the Mexican-American border, and the required training of U.S. Army Apache helicopter pilots,'' Jenny asked, ''as less strenuous than what you're doing here?''

Tunneling her fingers through her loose, slightly wavy hair, Dallas said, ''Absolutely. That will be fun compared to the nonstop tension that we operate under here.''

''The mission requires someone with a lot of diplomacy. I note here from our mission analysis that the person chosen for this assignment must be able to get along with men even though there will be prejudice against a woman being in command of the training.'' Jenny looked up. ''Are you prepared for the male Apache pilots to give you problems because you're a woman, Dallas?''

She leaned forward, her elbow on her knee. ''That's a good question, Jenny. My answer is yes,

I can. After all, I'm an Israeli pilot on loan to the U.S. Army. I went through Apache rotorcraft training at Fort Rucker, Alabama, some time ago. We had a *lot* of prejudice thrown against us because we were the first class of women to go through that male bastion. We learned well from that experience.'' She smiled slightly, then her eyes narrowed. ''I believe my age, which is twenty-nine, and my three years of experience in a combat zone, will eventually get these younger pilots to come around and respect me and what I have to teach them. They might not like the fact that I'm a woman. But they will respect the fact that I'm a combat veteran. It's one thing to have been in the two-day Gulf War. It's completely another to be operating daily on a wartime footing such as we have here, and live to tell about it.''

''I see. And why would you want to put yourself into the same situation that you endured before with U.S. Army Apache helicopter pilots?''

Dallas grinned and leaned back, relaxed. ''You're very good at asking the right questions,'' she murmured. ''You should be an XO.''

Laughing, Jenny nodded and blushed. ''Thank you.'' She glanced over to see admiration shining in Matt's eyes, and an I-told-you-so look on his face. ''But I don't think I have the moxie, the courage that you women display here daily every time you fly against those Kamov Black Sharks that are just waiting to try and destroy you." Shaking her head, Jenny patted the laptop. "I'll stick to being an interviewer, fair enough?"

Dallas smiled fully. "Okay…suit yourself. We can always use someone like you down here, though. Your insight and perceptions are bang on, and in my job as XO, I'm more a personnel manager than anything else, making sure things work smoothly and fluidly around here. You have that same kind of people awareness in you. And that's a gift an XO needs just as much as training."

Glowing inwardly, Jenny nodded. "Thanks, Dallas. And do you see your abilities to handle and manage people as one of the reasons why you want this mission?"

"Yes. I feel I can smooth over rough spots, and I can deal with challenge and adversity better than most." She grinned a little more widely. "I was raised in a kibbutz in Israel. My father was a military pilot."

"And he was highly decorated," Jenny noted, looking at the personnel record.

"Yes. And my mother is in the Mossad, the secret service of our country."

"So, you come from a military family."

"If you live in Israel, the military is a fundamental part of your life, Jenny. Everyone gives two mandatory years to it."

"What made you want to become a combat helicopter pilot? Over in Israel, they have no women in that arm of their air force.''

"Exactly." Dallas pursed her lips. "I was born to fly. Growing up, I remember seeing the eagles and hawks around our kibbutz. I wanted to soar, to feel the lift of that hot desert air taking me up into the blue of the sky." She aimed her hand upward. "My father was a military jet pilot. He taught me to fly when I was fourteen years old. Later, I grew to love helicopters, and by the time I was eighteen, I had hundreds of hours flying them. It was natural for me to want to fly helos. He suggested I apply to the U.S. Army, as part of their foreign pilot exchange program, for training." With a shrug, she said, "I got lucky…well, maybe that isn't the right word. My father, because of who he is, was able to open that door for me. The U.S. Army allowed me to come and train, and that's where I met Maya. After we received our wings, I applied to come down here to be a part of this clandestine operation. They accepted me and the rest is history."

"That is so impressive," Jenny murmured. "You've done so much to open up the possibilities for women in Israel to fly combat."

"I hope so." Dallas smiled warmly. She looked at the watch on her wrist. "I'm sorry, I've got to go—I've got to be at a tact and strat meeting in five minutes. Do you have any other questions?" she asked as she rose.

Jenny nodded. "Just one. Why are you called Dallas and not by your real name, Sarah?"

Chuckling, Dallas halted at the door, her hand resting on the jamb. "Oh, that. I think you know every pilot gets a nickname or handle during flight school?"

"Yes."

"Do you remember the American television series, *Dallas*?"

"Of course."

Her eyes crinkled with amusement. "In my younger days, I had this wild obsession about the American West. Cowboys. Indians. And my favorite show was *Dallas*. So my women squad mates chose the handle Dallas for me."

"Have you been to Texas? To Dallas?" Jenny wondered with a smile.

"Oh, yes." She rolled her eyes. "That's another story, for another day." Lifting her hand, she said, "Thanks for taking the time to see me. I'll keep my fingers crossed that you'll consider me for that training opening up on the border."

After she left, Jenny turned to Matt. "What a difference in personalities!"

He sat up and put his coffee mug on the edge of her desk. "You're seeing the difference between just being a pilot in the squadron, like Akiva, and someone whose collateral duties are much more

critical. Being a CO or XO are the two hardest positions to be in.''

''What is your feeling about Dallas?''

Matt grinned. ''Judging from the shining look,
the excitement in your eyes, I'd say you've found
the perfect woman to head up that border mission.''

Touching her cheek, Jenny mumbled, ''I can't
hide a thing from you, can I?''

Gloating, he said, ''No…but you know by now
that whatever you reveal is safe with me.'' More
than anything, Matt wanted Jenny to feel comfortable around him. This morning, when he'd held her
as she sobbed out her heart to him, he knew that
they'd taken an important step in that direction.
He'd held her. He hadn't tried to take advantage of
the situation. Oh, it was hell on him, no doubt about
it. Even now he positively itched to slide his fingers
around her smooth, small breast, to nuzzle his face
into her sweet-smelling, silky blond hair, or kiss the
nape of her slender neck, which probably would feel
like a soft, fuzzy peach beneath his lips. It was a
damn good thing she couldn't read his mind. And
even better that he could put an unreadable mask
across his face so she couldn't discern the lurid,
selfish, greedy thoughts he had about her.

Reaching out, Jenny touched Matt's hand, which
rested on the side of the desk near his coffee cup.
''You make me feel safe,'' she said quietly. ''This

morning, when I cried…you have no idea how wonderful it felt to be in your arms… to be held….''

"I'll always be a safe harbor for you, Jenny," Matt replied, gazing at her intently. "And that means beyond the scope of this mission. We've been thrown together for now, but I'd like to think that when we get home, what we've got, what we've shared, won't be over."

There, he'd said it. He'd put his biggest hopes into words. Judging by the widening look in her blue eyes, the way her black pupils enlarged, Matt knew he'd struck a sensitive chord in Jenny. Her thin blond brows knitted for a moment and, hands fluttering, she busied herself with the files. Matt knew her well enough by now to know that was a nervous reaction. Her brows dipped and her mouth went thin. What was she thinking? Feeling? Had he gone too far? Probably. *Damn.*

Licking her lips nervously, Jenny cast him a quick glance. "Gosh, Matt…everything seems so crazy for me right now, so different…." Her heart pounded at the idea that Matt wanted to continue to explore their relationship once this was over. She was thunderstruck by that. Hope warred with the silly idealism that she brought to every relationship. In her experience, Jenny had found she'd expected too much from the man. And yet Matt's sincerity, the burning look in his eyes, made her heart skitter with such elation that she could not ignore it.

Muttering, he said, "Yeah…I didn't mean to pressure you, Jenny."

Before he could say another word, the intruder alarm bell rang noisily throughout the cave complex. He saw Jenny jump in response to the loud, harsh sound, and then physically force herself to sit and relax in the aftermath.

Mind and heart in tumult over Matt's admission, Jenny didn't know what else to do or say at the moment. Lamely, she offered, "There goes our next interview," and she held up the personnel file of Chief Warrant Officer Cam Anderson, a green-eyed, redheaded twenty-five-year-old from Montana.

"She's got the duty?"

Nodding, Jenny stood up. "Yes, and so does the other perspective volunteer, Captain Dove Rivera." She hesitated, deep in thought over his declaration. How often had she dreamed of a man saying those wonderful words to her?

Standing, he said, "Might as well call it a day, then? There's no telling how long they'll be gone." Giving her a glance, he saw Jenny standing there, a pensive look on her face, the file clasped in her hands.

"Yes, we might as well fly back to Agua Caliente," she murmured.

Matt smiled slightly as he met and held her blue eyes. Was Jenny going to dodge his admission? It looked like it. Disappointment flowed through him.

Looking at his watch, he stated, "It's almost noon. How about a picnic down by the Urubamba River? Maria was telling me yesterday about a sweet spot with plenty of shade that's ideal. It's close to Agua Caliente, too. How about it?"

"A picnic?" Jenny liked the idea and drowned in the burning look he gave her.

Seeing the interest and excitement in her eyes as she placed the laptop in her black nylon carrying case, Matt said, "Yeah. Are you game?"

"Just you and me?"

"Yes." He saw the corners of her mouth pull upward. "Am I pushing you?" His heart thudded hard in his chest as he asked the question. If Jenny felt pressured, then it was a no go as far as he was concerned.

Zipping the case shut, Jenny lifted her chin and gazed the short distance to where he stood, his brow wrinkled with concern. "I'd love to, Matt." And she would. Her heart skittered. Where was this leading? He was so incredibly handsome, strong and self-assured. Why would he see anything in her? And then Jenny caught herself and stopped that old tape from the past from playing itself out in her head. No, she was worthy of someone like Matt Davis. She told herself that sternly a number of times as she shut off the light and left the office with him. A part of her did believe there was hope for them—a very small part. Another part of her

wondered whether such a dream could ever come
true. And then the sick, wounded side of her that
had yet to heal said that she was being a fool once
again, that she wasn't worthy and that he was only
after her to get her into bed for a one-night stand.

As they walked down the hall, Jenny's heart lifted
with joy. Euphoria swept over her. Suddenly, the
healing part of her *did* believe that Matt was genuinely interested in her, warts and all. Even a toad
with warts could have a lifelong mate, she reminded
herself as she took the metal grate stairs down to
the black lava floor of the cave. As they walked
toward an awaiting golf cart that would zip them
through the tunnel to the mining side of the mountain and the world beyond, Jenny smiled. It was the
smile of a woman finding the door to her prison,
opening it and walking outside for the first time in
her life.

"Llama cheese sandwiches," Matt murmured ap-
preciatively as he reached out and handed Jenny the
huge slices of dark brown bread stuffed with peeled
tomatoes and white, crumbly cheese. He had
brought one of the old wool army blankets along
and they had just settled comfortably on it to enjoy
their picnic. Thanks to Maria's directions, they'd located the small sandy spot beneath the protective
branches of a silver-barked eucalyptus tree towering
on the bank. A hundred feet away, the Urubamba

splashed and thundered. There were gargantuan boulders of all colors and sizes out in the river, large enough that they couldn't be swept away by the strong, relentless current. The river actually looked like a garden of stones more than water. Over the eons, the boulders had tumbled from cliffs in the rugged Andes, from which the Urubamba was born. The sky had cleared to a powder-blue hue, and was strewn with hundreds of cobalt-colored swallows with cream breasts, flitting and diving along the restless, churning river, snapping up dragonflies, mosquitoes and moths unlucky enough to be spotted by the birds.

Jenny took the sandwich in both hands. "This is huge! I can't possibly eat all of it, Matt." Kannie and Patrick, the owners of India Feliz, had ordered their chef to make them a "wonderful" picnic lunch. Wonderful it was—and huge.

"Eat what you can," Matt said, setting out the green bottle of Peruvian white wine. He popped the cork and poured the golden liquid into awaiting plastic cups. "Kannie tends to think you're too skinny." The woman had thoughtfully added tasty, thinly sliced, deep-fried potatoes with their special herbs and salt sprinkled across them. Matt could overdose on them, they were so good. But then, potatoes in Peru tasted like none other worldwide. This was, in his opinion, the potato capital of the world. And if that wasn't enough, Kannie had included two thick slices of chocolate cake with white frosting for dessert.

Munching on the delicious sandwich, Jenny sighed. She sat on one side of the blanket with her legs crossed, the picnic spread between her and Matt. The dappled shade of the eucalyptus above them cut the heat and humidity, which always increased between noon and sunset. The riverbank was about five to ten degrees cooler than the jungle itself because of the ice-fed stream churning and tumbling rebelliously in front of them. The water, as a matter of fact, had felt like ice cubes to Jenny, when she'd tested it earlier with her hands. She didn't see how Maria or any other Peruvian woman could constantly work in that chilling water from the tributary. Maybe that was why Maria's hands were so leathery and thick—to protect them from hypothermia.

Looking up at Matt as he eagerly bit into his own sandwich, Jenny gestured to the river. "I have never seen a river that rages like this one."

"This is what they call a '5' river," he told her. Taking one of the red linen napkins, he handed it to Jenny and then got one for himself. She looked so young and relaxed here by the water. A picnic had been the perfect idea. "Guys who run rapids rate rivers from 1 through 5," he told her. "The more dangerous it is—the faster it flows and the more rocks or boulders you have to try and navigate

around—the higher the number.'' With a shake of
his head, he sipped the fruity wine. ''Frankly, I consider anyone who even *thinks* of trying to run the
Urubamba insane. No one could do it. They'd kill
themselves with the speed this river has and end up
smashing into one of those huge boulders out
there.''

''No disagreement from me. Plus the water is so
cold, Matt.''

''That's why it's great trout fishing.'' He grinned.
''Trout thrive in icy water. I was born in Ketchum,
Idaho. My dad ran an outfitting company. I grew up
hiking and fishing all the time.'' His father had a
small company that he'd built into a multimillion-
dollar business.

''What a wonderful childhood.'' Jenny studied
the river for a long moment before speaking. ''Maria was telling me that a boy who works at a local
hotel was swept away in that tributary where they
wash their clothes. He slipped on a rock while carrying luggage across it with several other young
men. She said it happened so fast that no one reacted soon enough. The boy was dragged out into
the center by the strong current, and in no time was
washed out into the Urubamba.'' Her voice lowered.
''Maria said they found his body three days later,
washed up far below the town. That's so sad, but
that tributary and this river are nothing to mess
with.'' She shivered.

"I'm not going to argue that point at all," Matt murmured, taking another hefty bite of his sandwich. The sunlight played upon her blond hair, dappling it with spots that reminded him of gold coins. Jenny *was* a treasure to him. In all ways.

"Do you know how long it's been since I took time out for a picnic? Just to sit and watch the world go by?" he asked.

She smiled and sipped her wine. "No. Tell me."

Stretching out to his full length, his legs off the blanket and resting across some small, smooth rocks, he said, "I can't remember the last time. When I was growing up I used to like to go down to the creek on our property, go fishing and just lie under that big, spreading oak's arms."

"Sounds nice," she ventured. "You look like you wish for more of that now?"

"You're astute."

"Thank you. Well? Are you wanting to rest from your dangerous, intense lifestyle? To just spend time watching the world go by?"

Matt's mouth pulled slightly as he popped several salty slices of potatoes into his mouth. "Yeah, maybe I am. I'm older now. Feeling like I want to settle down."

"And before?"

"Footloose and fancy free, as they say. That's probably what destroyed my first marriage."

"Being away so often?" Jenny knew that many

of the missions Perseus ran were three to six months in length. Sometimes longer, especially undercover ops. And that was a long time to be gone unless there was a very understanding spouse at the other end, which wasn't often the case.

Nodding, Matt sipped the wine and then set it down in front of him on the blanket. "Yeah, my being gone really put the marriage on the skids. Everything else that helped push it over the edge was secondary. When I finally 'got it'—that my being gone so often and so long was really at the core of our problems, I tried to change. But—" he scowled "—it was too late, only I didn't want to admit it. I had quit the SEALs and joined Perseus, thinking that it would somehow save what we had. But...it didn't."

"Life from where I stand is an endless classroom," Jenny told him gently. "We all make tons of mistakes. It's what we do with what we learn from them the next time around that counts."

"Wise words from a wise young woman," he granted as he finished off the sandwich. Reaching for the chocolate cake, he removed the plastic film. Taking a plastic fork, he dug into it.

The silence stretched between them. It wasn't really silence with the roar of the Urubamba right next to them. Matt enjoyed watching Jenny eat. She took small bites. After every bite, she'd suck on her fingertips, which got messy with the llama cheese. Of late, he'd noticed that a lot of her restlessness and frenetic, almost manic activity, had ceased. She seemed much calmer. Happier. Or was it his imagination? Was it him? Peru? Or was she becoming more confident in herself and her skills as these interviews progressed? Matt wasn't sure. Finally, he got up enough courage to ask her a question that had been begging to be voiced for a long time.

"Jenny?"

"Yes?"

"What are your dreams? What do you want out of life? Where do you see yourself five years from now?"

Chapter Nine

Jenny thought for a moment and then slowly wiped her fingers a final time on the red linen napkin. She saw the seriousness and interest in Matt's eyes and knew that his question wasn't small talk. Her heart skittered, and she was unable to drag her gaze from the tender flame burning in his gray eyes.

"Well...you know, I never had a template for my life." With a slight shrug, she continued, "Maybe being passed around to different families was upsetting to me and I just never got attached to anything...or hardly anyone. But I knew I wanted to make something of myself, come heck or high water. I had to prove to myself that I'm not the dummy they called me all through the different schools I went to. Getting that degree was really my only goal.''

Looking toward the roaring, massive Urubamba, Jenny said with deprecation, ''My life has been like that river, in a lot of ways, Matt. Look at all those huge boulders, hundreds of them, scattered across the expanse. I feel like I've been a Ping-Pong ball, hitting life's boulders and being bounced to the next ever since I was a child.'' Her mouth curved ruefully as she turned and met his hooded gaze. ''And if I ever fell in that river, I'd be bounced around like one, too.''

''Perish the thought,'' Matt growled. ''You wouldn't last five minutes in it. No one would. Not even me, and I'm a trained SEAL. If smashing full speed into one of those boulders didn't kill you outright, then the hypothermia would get you in ten minutes or less.''

Slowly folding the napkin in her lap and then smoothing it out against her thighs, Jenny said, ''No argument there. Anyway…my goals? Dreams? I just kinda hang loose, you know? Getting this job and working for Morgan was an unexpected joy. I love him so much. He's like a gruff old teddy bear, sorta growly, but he has such a tender, caring side to him. And Laura…well, she's wonderful.'' Giving him a slight smile, Jenny added in a whisper, ''Sometimes…sometimes in a moment of weakness, I fantasize that Laura and Morgan are my *real* mother and father. Oh, I know that's stupid...but that's how I feel toward them. And because of how they treat me, kind of like another daughter, I want to stay with Perseus for as long as they'll have me. Morgan giving me a chance to take this assignment is a huge plum, I know. I don't want to screw it up. I want to do well and show him that his faith in me is justified.''

''Jenny, you're not going to screw up this mission. You can see now that you're good at what you do. I know Morgan will be happy with how you're handling everything, and who you choose for these three missions.''

Nodding, she moved her finger in a circle on the napkin. ''Yes...I'm beginning to see that.'' Lifting her chin, Jenny beamed at him. ''Thanks to you... and to the pilots who, in their own way, support and encourage me, too.''

''Well deserved,'' Matt murmured. ''What about your personal life? You've told me what you want careerwise, what about the private Jenny Wright? What are her dreams? Her yearnings?''

Closing her eyes, she smiled and clasped her hands in her lap. ''Oh! What a dreamer I am!''

''Can you share some of them with me?'' Matt sat very still. Jenny looked in that moment like a golden angel as the sunlight lanced across her hair, stirred by the breeze along the river. The expression of joy on her face expanded his heart. How badly he wanted to rise up on his knees, lean across that basket and plant a hot kiss on those smiling lips of hers.

"I *love* being a part-time baby-sitter for Laura. I love children. Well…" Jenny opened her eyes and laughed "…you can see that by how much I adore Daniel and the other children here in this town. I'd love to have a family of my own someday." Her brows moved downward. "I'd like to have a chance to undo what was done to me, and to give my children a stable, secure, caring environment. I'd like to have a man who *wants* to be a father, not just someone who comes home at night and is available on weekends to his kids." Opening her hands, she added wryly, "I know this is a dream. I know it's not reality. But I see Morgan and Laura. He's over at their house almost every noon, for an hour. And sometimes, when things aren't hectic, Laura will bring the twins to see him on weekends if he's got to work over there. She makes sure he's not pressed for time. I love to see Peter and Kelly, who are twelve now. They're curious and fascinated with the HQ being underground. They love all the big screen displays that show the satellites, and the colorful pictures that show where across the globe our mission teams are located."

"So, you want a man who's really involved in raising the kids?"

"Absolutely. Otherwise, why have them? Why put it all on the woman to raise them, while he gets to be an absentee dad? I don't agree with that, Matt. I'm probably expecting too much of a man I might want to marry someday, but it's too important to gloss over. I won't do that to a child. I see how wonderful Katy—their second child, who's seventeen now—has turned out, with Morgan's daily influence on her. She's such a stunning and beautiful young woman. She looks so much like Laura.''

"Jason is a little different," Matt noted as he sipped his wine.

"Well," Jenny said worriedly, "you know he was kidnapped by a drug lord when he was very young? Although he was rescued over in Hawaii by two of Morgan's best, he was old enough to remember those events, and I'm sure it's scarred him. He was torn from his family. Held hostage. And even though he's nineteen years old now, and going into his second year at the Naval Academy as a midshipman, Jason is withdrawn. Being firstborn, he's following in his dad's footsteps and wants to become a marine upon graduation. But he isn't trusting and open like the other three children. I can understand why. I wasn't stolen out of my house by a drug lord, but I was passed from one family to another, and the feelings are the same—like being abandoned.''

"I think you're right about Jas," Matt said as he

set the empty glass aside. "There's a lot of turmoil deep inside him. He's become a loner as a result and doesn't trust anyone or anything outside himself."

"I know." She sighed unhappily. "I watched Morgan and Laura when he came home for the Easter holiday. They love him so much. They want him to be happy, but he isn't. Somehow, since that kidnapping, some deep connection between Jas and his parents has been broken. It's so sad, Matt, to see him. I wanted to cry. Jas just went off to his room, to be alone. And when Laura tried to get him involved in the family Easter egg hunt, he went for a hike into the mountains, instead."

"The boy has emotional wounds," Matt agreed. "Maybe being at the academy will help him understand commitment and teamwork. At least, we can hope that."

"Yes, and that as he gets older and experiences more of life's hard knocks, he'll be able to get in touch with his emotions and feelings and bond again with Morgan and Laura. I know, from being a psychologist, that on some unconscious level, Jas blames his parents for being kidnapped and abandoned. He's got a lot of unconscious rage aimed at them because of it. I'm sure he's not aware it's there or that he even understands his actions are hurting everyone. It's only natural for a small child to see separation from his parents as some sort of punishment. And no matter how much love, praise and support Morgan and Laura have lavished on Jason since his rescue, he's rejected it. The experience made him feel too vulnerable, and he's built a hellacious armored wall around himself to keep that from ever happening again.''

''Did your childhood affect you that way, Jenny?'' Matt said, enjoying the way the corners of her mouth lifted at his observation.

''No. But although I felt abandoned like Jason did, I wasn't kidnapped, and there's the difference. I mean, poor little Jas was literally snatched out of his bed. During the rescue, Sabra, the woman operative, held him, while Craig Talbot, the helicopter pilot, flew them out of the drug lord's villa. Only the helicopter was shot up and they crash-landed halfway to their destination. Jas had to endure that trauma, too. Sabra used her own body to shield him after they made the emergency landing. And if she hadn't run away from the site with him, Jason would have been killed.''

Shrugging, Jenny said more softly, ''Jas remembers all of it. And what's worse, he considered Sabra his 'auntie'—he was very close to her as a young one. That's why Morgan put her on that mission to locate and extract him. Sabra was wounded by a piece of flying shrapnel when the helicopter blew up. Jas was found sitting next to her, crying his little eyes out, while she was bloody and unconscious.''

Shivering, Jenny gave Matt a soulful look. "He's endured a lot. Those kinds of memories are like a brand on your heart and brain, as far as I'm concerned. They are life-altering events that affect a person forever."

Nodding, Matt said, "Jason has suffered a lot, there's no question. Maybe being in the naval academy will help him. He so badly wants to carry on the family's military tradition. I think he wants to erase the stain on the family's honor, too."

"Oh...that." Jenny sighed and sipped her wine with pleasure. "I think Morgan has more than shown the American public that he wasn't the traitor they thought he was during the Vietnam War."

"Still," Matt said, "I saw it in Jas's eyes sometimes in the year before he left for the academy. You know Laura and Morgan throw a huge, five-day Christmas party every year for those of us home from missions at the time."

She smiled. "Oh, yes! Laura goes all out. She loves to entertain and see people have a good time. She knows the stresses and demands on the mercs and their families. I helped her with some of the decorating last year, and drove to Helena with her to shop for gifts. The celebration was a lot of fun, and I got to meet a number of people who work for Perseus."

Matt's eyes crinkled. "I missed the last one because I was out on a mission, but I heard from a number of the guys who were able to attend that it was the best ever. The women mercs like it because they got to dress up.''

Sighing, Jenny said, "It was wonderful, Matt. I loved it. Laura is so good at pulling people out of their shells and getting them to mix and mingle. Morgan is good, too, but Laura's heart and soul goes into this extravaganza. For five days, we were wined and dined while we celebrated and danced the nights away. On Christmas morning, they opened up their beautiful log house to about fifty people or so. There was a huge twenty-foot-tall Christmas tree, which we all helped to decorate on the first evening, and then everyone gathered for brunch. Afterward, we got to open gifts." She clapped her hands with delight. "You wouldn't believe how wonderful it was! Laura knows every person who works for Perseus—and what they would like. It was great to see men and women who risk their lives become like animated children during the celebration. There was so much laughter and warmth. I just loved it. Laura calls it her Five Days of Christmas celebration.''

"And seeing the glimmer in your eyes, I can tell you're a big kid at Christmas yourself." It was one of the many things Matt had come to appreciate about Jenny. When she needed to be an adult, she was. But the moment she could slip out of those traces, she became spontaneous and childlike, filled with awe and wonder at the world around her. He found that refreshing and realized she made him feel more like a kid himself.

Laughing pleasantly, Jenny reached for her cake, unwrapped it and eagerly began to consume it. "That's one thing I really like about myself—being able to be a kid still. Maybe that's why I love children so much. They haven't lost the ability to be flexible and spontaneous in the moment."

He regarded her from beneath his short, thick lashes. "So, we're back to my original question, Jenny Wright. What do you want out of life?"

Hesitating fractionally, Jenny placed the plate in her lap, her hands around it. "The same thing everyone wants. I'd like to be married someday. I'd love to have two kids."

"Would you balance career and kids?" Matt asked.

Jenny shrugged. "I feel very strongly that children need a full-time mother for the first seven years of their life. I got to experience both sides of this. I had some foster mothers who stayed at home full-time. I had others that worked full-time, along with my foster fathers, while I had a procession of baby-sitters."

"You've been able to develop a unique perspective on this," Matt noted. He saw Jenny frown.

"I've thought a lot about this…I chew everything to death," she admitted with a giggle. "I'd hope that my husband would make enough money to allow me to stay home with our child. If he didn't, then I'd try to have some kind of job I could do at home, so I'd be there, anyway. And if that didn't work, then I'd look at taking a night job so I could at least be there during the day for the baby.'' Her brows rose and she gave him a playful look. ''Of course, the dad would be hauling his fair share of the load of raising this child, too. It wouldn't all be on my shoulders. He'd learn how to wash the baby, change diapers and care for him or her just as I would.''

''That's a fair expectation,'' Matt agreed.

''What about you?'' Jenny asked, spooning more of the delicious cake into her mouth.

''Me?'' Matt shrugged and played with the napkin in front of him. ''After my divorce, I swore I'd never marry again. But now…I guess age and time have worn me down on that statement.'' He grinned a little. ''I don't like the loneliness, to be honest. I don't like coming off a mission, going to the condo in Philipsburg where the mercs stay between assignments. The condo is beautiful and has all the amenities…but it's lonely.''

Finishing off the cake, Jenny placed the paper plate and wrapper back into the pack. ''That's the great thing about a good marriage. You have your best friend to do things with, to talk to, to share with.''

"Yes, and in a bad marriage, none of those things are in place."

"You speak from experience," Jenny offered gently, seeing his gray eyes darken with old pain from the past. Reaching out, she squeezed his hand, which rested on top of the crinkled linen napkin between them. "Looking at how marriages are so disposable nowadays, I think a key to a successful one is that you become best friends, that you share a love of things together."

Turning his hand over, he lifted her fingers and pressed a tender kiss to the backs of them. Her eyes flared with surprise, and then turned languid with pleasure. Smiling up at her as he reluctantly released her hand, Matt asked, "Can we be friends?"

Jenny smiled in response. It was almost too much to hope for! Matt wanted her friendship. The thought filled her with happiness—and, she mused, a flutter of anticipation. What would it be like to *really* get to know Matt?

Jenny sat expectantly behind her desk at the Black Jaguar Base. Chief Warrant Officer Two, twenty-five-year-old Camilla Anderson, was due any minute for her interview. Matt sat in a relaxed position in the chair near the wall, coffee in hand. He gave Jenny a slight smile.

Matt thought Jenny looked even more beautiful this morning. Had the picnic down by the river done it? His kissing her hand? Or maybe he felt that way because they had finally taken the time to sit and explore one another on a deeper personal level? The answer was probably all of the above. Today she wore a pale pink, short-sleeved cotton blouse with a colorful scarf around her neck, khaki shorts and her hiking boots. Her hair was slightly mussed, as it always seemed to be, but on her it looked fetching. There was always a chaotic energy about Jenny, but he was growing to enjoy that aspect of her. Her hair, he realized now, seemed to symbolize her restless nature. She tried to tame it into place, but something—the helicopter blades, the mountain breeze— was always thwarting her efforts, and finally she'd give up let it be tousled and windblown—and lovely.

Maybe that was the key to Jenny, he mused, as he sipped the hot, fragrant coffee. Letting her be who she was. Two immature men had hurt her by trying to force her into a mold of what they thought she should be instead of prizing her as the unique flower she was.

Last night had been pure, unadulterated hell on Matt. She had slept soundly, like a baby, beside him. And he'd barely slept at all, inhaling the scent of the spicy ginger shampoo she'd used to wash her hair earlier. How badly he'd wanted to reach out, slide his arms around her and bring her against him.

Still, Matt acknowledged that simply sleeping together was helping Jenny. Each night she was less and less restless. She slept more deeply. Those dark circles beneath her eyes had disappeared and she was blooming like one of the breathtaking orchids that grew in such proliferation all around Agua Caliente.

CWO2 Camille Anderson came thunking down the hall toward the opened door, interrupting Matt's thoughts. As he shifted his attention to the Apache helicopter pilot who raced in the door, breathless, the young woman gave them a quick smile of hello and took the seat in front of the desk.

"Whew! Sorry I'm almost late." She glanced at the watch on her left wrist. "I've got collateral duty in the maintenance section with Major York, and we ran into some problems with one of the Apaches... thing unexpected." Blowing out a breath of air, she quickly moved her fingers through her thick, naturally curly auburn hair.

smiled and said, "Don't worry about it. We've learned that things around here are like a cork bobbing on the ocean, and we've got to be flexible."

Cam grinned and nodded. She smoothed her black uniform across her long, strong-looking thighs. "Yes, ma'am, that's the name of the game."

"Call me Jenny. What do you like to be called?"

"Cam." She grinned broadly. "Or you can call

me 'Tree Trimmer,' which is my new handle around here.''

Smiling, Jenny said, "Tree Trimmer? What kind of a name is that?"

Opening her long, artistic-looking hands, Cam laughed deeply. "About two years ago, I put the skids of our old Cobra, when we still had it, into the tops of the jungle trees and whacked off a bunch of branches. There was a thunderstorm approaching, and a gust of wind, a strong one, pushed the helicopter downward. I compensated for it, but not soon enough, and we ended up eating some jungle real estate. Major Stevenson was with me at the time, and gave me the name."

Jenny smiled. She liked the tall pilot. Cam Anderson had lively forest-green eyes, a square face and short auburn hair that barely stayed tucked behind her ears. The ruddiness of her cheeks and the hundreds of freckles sprinkled across her fine, thin nose made her look decidedly Irish. There was a quiet alertness about Cam. Five foot nine inches tall, she was solidly built and large-boned. Glancing at her file, Jenny saw that she weighed a hundred fifty-five pounds. She was all legs, Jenny realized, with wide hips. In the back of her mind, Jenny applauded women who carried some weight on them. This skinny-as-a-rail stuff was for the birds. Cam was physically strong-looking, and Jenny knew that, like all the pilots and most of the other women personnel of the base, she worked out at the gym that was set up on the mining side.

"What was your handle before you turned those trees into salad?" Jenny teased with a smile. She saw Cam brighten as she sat before her, both booted feet on the floor, her hands relaxed on her thighs.

"Coming out of Fort Rucker training, they called me Cougar." She shrugged, a grin edging her wide mouth. "I come from Montana. I was born up in the Rocky Mountains. We have cougars and black bears all over that area. When I was very young, my mother had left me out in our backyard, which butted up against the national forest. When she came back a few minutes later, she saw a cougar sitting no more than ten feet away from me. Just watching me."

"Goodness," Jenny exclaimed. "I'll bet your mother just about had a heart attack!"

"I was six at the time. I still remember the incident. I wasn't scared, either. I kept saying, 'Here, kitty, kitty, kitty!' and that's what freaked my mother out."

"Amazing. What happened next?"

Cam grinned. "The cougar leaped up and left as soon as she saw my mother running toward me."

"Was it going to eat you?"

Cam's eyes lightened with laughter. "No, I don't think so. I still remember the feeling of that meeting.

It was like seeing an old friend again, odd as that sounds. I was happy to see the cougar.''

Jenny touched her cheek. ''I feel for your poor mother. She must have thought the worst.''

''Oh, my mother was pretty cool about it. I remember her picking me up and saying that the cougar was too big to be a house cat and that I shouldn't try calling it, because it wouldn't come. That it belonged in the wild.''

Jenny smiled. ''Is that how you see yourself, Cam? A woman who belongs in the wild?''

''Great question. Yes, I do. I've always been very confident about myself, and that's probably due to my parents telling me from the earliest I can remember that I could do anything I wanted in life, and be successful at it.''

''Good for them,'' Jenny murmured, writing down the information to be put into her laptop later. ''So tell me why you want to volunteer for one of these three assignments.''

Cam became very serious. She crossed one leg and frowned. ''I'm going to level with you, Jenny. It will probably cost me the possibility of getting one of these missions, but I owe you—and Major Stevenson—the truth on why I'd like to be considered.''

Jenny saw pain in Cam's eyes and in the way her mouth thinned. ''I'm listening.''

With a heavy sigh, Cam opened her hands and

lowered her voice. "A year ago Major Stevenson and I were flying the Cobra on a mapping mission, looking for new trails that the druggies were cutting in order to get their cocaine to drop-off points. We were at tree height." Her voice turned sad. "We got attacked by a Kamov out of the blue. Neither of us saw it coming. It shot us down."

Jenny frowned. "Oh, dear…"

"Yeah," Cam muttered, "bad news. *Really* bad news. I'm sure you've heard this already…it's an old story around the base."

"What story?"

One of Cam's thick brows moved upward. "How I abandoned Maya after the crash? The druggies were coming. I could see them in their trucks, high-tailing it toward us. The Cobra was burning a hundred feet away from us. I managed to drag Maya out of the burning helo because she was unconscious. She'd taken a hit on the helmet from a branch as the helo twisted and fell down through the trees." Rubbing her face, she muttered, "Damn, this is harder than I thought it would be. Anyway…" she sighed with resignation "…I abandoned Maya. I ran away. I ran into the jungle to escape the druggies who were coming."

Jenny's heart contracted. She saw the anguish in Cam's face and heard it in her husky, low voice. Slanting Matt a quick glance, she saw him grimly studying the pilot. Although his face was unreadable, Jenny could feel he was suffering for Cam, as well.

"Wait…" Jenny murmured, holding up her hand. "No, I haven't heard this story from anyone, Cam. And I don't have the kind of military background to judge your decision."

"I do," Matt stated quietly. He set the coffee mug on the desk and folded his hands between his thighs as he studied Cam. "You might give Jenny your reasons for what you did, Cam. I think I know, but you need to share it with her so she understands the context of your decision—why you decided to do what you did under those circumstances."

Nodding, Cam blew out a painful breath of air. "Right…of course." She turned her attention back to Jenny. "I had a military decision to make. Maya was my commander. You've seen how thick the jungle is, right?"

"Yes, it's very dense, nearly impossible to walk through," Jenny replied. "I've heard the only way you can get through it is to hack a path with a machete."

"Correct," Cam whispered. "Well, Maya was out cold. The druggies were less than a quarter mile away and coming at high speed down that dirt road toward us. I knew they would capture both of us. I also knew that no one here at the base knew we'd been knocked out of the sky. I—I had a decision to make—leave Maya or try and take her with me."

"But," Jenny said quickly, "if she was unconscious, how in the world could you carry her through that wall of jungle? That would be impossible."

Nodding, Cam whispered, "That was the dilemma I faced. I wasn't hurt except for my arm being injured. I could get away. I felt I could escape deep enough into the jungle and eventually, over a day or two, make it back to the base to tell them what had happened. From there, we could mount a rescue effort for Maya."

"Under the circumstances," Jenny said gently, "I don't see that you had any choice in the matter. Did you escape?"

"Yes…reluctantly, let me tell you." After rubbing her face, Cam dropped her hands and stared down at the floor between her black flight boots. "I've never felt so horrible…leaving Maya. I didn't know how badly hurt she really was. I knew, from a military perspective, the right thing to do was get out, but damn…I didn't want to leave my fallen comrade in harm's way. I didn't want to leave Maya in the hands of druggies who I knew could hurt or kill her."

Jenny's heart contracted with anguish for Cam, whose face was tense with torment. "I don't see that you had a choice."

"Well," Cam said quietly, "that's why I'm here. Eventually, I did get found by Major York and Wild

Woman, and I got lifted out of the jungle and taken back to the base, where I told them what had happened. Lucky for us, things worked out okay in the end, and Maya freed herself eventually…but it still hurts here.'' She pressed her hand to her heart region. ''I still feel like I abandoned her. My head tells me that what I did was right. But I was taught never to leave someone who was sick or hurt. And I feel that I should have stayed with her….'' She compressed her lips and gave Jenny a quick look.

''And that's why you want to volunteer for one of these missions? In some way, to make up for that incident?''

''Bingo. You got it.'' Cam straightened up and threw back her proud shoulders, as if to try and shrug off the invisible weight she carried to this day. ''I want a shot at one of those missions. I want to somehow make up for the past. I know Maya would be proud of me, maybe forgive me, if I could be successful at one of them. And that's what I'd like—a shot at the night border work. I have a lot of reasons to do it, to show her that she can have renewed faith and trust in me.''

''I see…'' Jenny murmured. ''I'll take your desire to make things right once again into consideration, Cam.''

She brightened. ''Thanks…it would mean a lot to me. I owe the major. I'd really like to repay her this way.''

Chapter Ten

Jenny gave Matt a searching look after Cam left. She got up and quietly shut the door to their office. Turning, she leaned against it, her arms across her breasts.

"I'd value your feedback on her, on the reasons she states, Matt. Right now, I don't feel Cam's the right person for that border mission."

He stood up and rubbed his jaw while he gazed out the small window that overlooked the rear of the cave. "You're not wrong to feel that way," he murmured. Turning, he moved to the front of the desk and sat down on the edge, his hands resting on the cool metal. Jenny looked concerned, and he could see the frustration in her eyes.

"Cam is fueled by guilt," he told her. "Guilt that would plague *any* military person, and that's what you need to put into perspective here. We're trained *never* to leave a fallen comrade in the field. It just isn't acceptable in the SEALs. The Marine Corps has a similar tradition. I really felt for her when she was sharing that experience with us. I'd be torn, too. But under the circumstances—" he hooked a thumb over his shoulder "—with that dense jungle out there, Cam wouldn't have gotten ten feet, carrying Maya over her shoulder. It's one thing to be able to move, it's a whole 'nother thing to be carrying an unconscious person. And at six foot tall, Maya isn't any lightweight."

"So, you think Cam did the right thing?"

Giving her a pained look, Matt said, "You know what? The only person who can really answer that is Cam. Her training told her not to leave Maya wounded, alone and in the hands of the enemy. Another part of her, the survivor, saw that if she didn't escape, then no one back at the base would even *begin* to have a clue as to what happened or where they were. At least if she escaped and made it back to base, there'd be *hope* that Maya could be rescued."

"I see both sides of the issue," Jenny murmured. "What would I do in her place, I wonder?"

Matt nodded. "Right. You have to put yourself in her shoes, with her training and mind-set. The other factor, which is the wild card in all this, is the personality involved. Frankly, knowing what I know about this incident from her, I'd say she made the correct call. Escape and live to fight another day. Escape to get word back to your team as to what happened, and then mount a rescue effort for the fallen comrade. I think she did the right thing. And as for her thinking Maya holds the decision against her, I know that's not correct. Cam is holding it against herself. Maya understood her decision—I know, because I talked to her about it earlier this week, when I saw Cam's name on the list. In fact, Maya has told Cam to her face that she'd have done exactly the same thing if she'd been in her shoes."

Jenny moved toward Matt, until she stood less than a foot away from him. The sleeves of his light blue chambray shirt were rolled up to just below his elbows, and the dark hair on his massive, well-muscled arms made her ache to reach out and slide her fingers across them. Fighting the urge, she studied his frowning features and darkened gray eyes as she pondered Cam's dilemma. "It's good to know you talked with Maya about this." She slanted him an amused glance. "If I was in trouble, you'd come after me, wouldn't you?"

Matt met her warm gaze. "Of course I would. And so would you, if the tables were turned."

Jenny nodded. "Yes, I would."

"Even if the deck was stacked against me? Even

knowing in advance that you might be killed in the process of trying to rescue me?''

"Without a doubt."

Matt gave her a long look. "People like you are the ones who, when a grenade from the enemy is rolled into a squad bay filled with people, throw themselves on it to save everyone else. But then, you die because of your actions."

"That is an act of ultimate courage—to put your life on the line for another, not knowing the outcome," Jenny agreed quietly as she chewed on her lower lip. She saw him roll his eyes. "What? What would you have done differently?"

"I'd probably kick the grenade out of the area with the toe of my boot, or pick it up and throw it. I'm not an idealist." Matt reached out and grazed her cheek, which instantly turned a flaming red. He saw the pleasure come to her eyes at his unexpected touch. How badly he wanted to kiss Jenny, to feel those soft lips beneath his hungry, greedy mouth. "You are."

Even though she was afraid, Jenny overcame her fear and boldly reached out and ruffled his hair in a playful motion. "You be the realist. I'm happy to be the idealist on our team."

Catching her hand, he smiled wolfishly. She grew still and relaxed within his warm, strong grasp. Matt saw the enjoyment, the gold flecks in her blue eyes as they glinted in merriment. With his other hand, he opened her smaller one and grazed her palm with his callused thumb. Instantly, he saw her lips part in surprise...and obvious pleasure.

"You know what?" he murmured as he held her tender gaze. "I like you just the way you are." Giving her hand a final squeeze, he released it. "Just don't find any grenades to go throw yourself on. I want you around me for a long, long time."

Shaken by his smoldering look and the grazing touch of his thumb upon her tingling palm, Jenny tried to smile, and failed miserably. "A 'fraidy cat? You want a mouse like me around? I don't believe it." She had said it partly in jest, part seriously.

"Then," Matt growled warningly, "believe this..." And he stood and placed his hands on her shoulders. Jenny looked up at him, surprise and desire written clearly in her eyes. Automatically, she placed her hands on his arms. Leaning down, he nuzzled her soft, silky hair, which smelled of wild ginger. "I want to kiss you so damn badly I ache, Jenny. But I won't do it...can't do it, unless you want me to." He rested his lips against her hair and felt her sudden intake of breath. Her hands hesitantly slid up to his elbows and she shyly leaned closer to him. There were scant inches between them now. Matt could feel the feminine heat of her body, the courageous heart beating beneath her small breasts.

Her world spun to a halt. Jenny hadn't expected

Matt to do this—to take her into his arms, to draw her so agonizingly close to his hard, male body. To press his mouth against her hair, so close to her left ear. She released the breath of trapped air from her lungs.

"I want you," he rasped unsteadily. "For all the right reasons, darlin'. You're precious to me, do you hear?" He slid his hands across her shoulders and forced himself not to pull her hard against him. This had to be mutual or it would never work. His heart was spilling over and he wasn't sure why. Maybe it was Cam's tortured story. Maybe he was fearful of losing Jenny because she was such an idealist. She'd give her life in a moment if need be, and he knew it. And then she'd be gone. Ripped out of his life forever. As a mercenary, as a SEAL, Matt knew how quickly life could be snuffed out. How fast it could be taken away from a person. His heart thundered in his chest with his desire to make her his now, immediately.

Jenny felt Matt's warm breath against the side of her face. She hungrily absorbed the feel of his roughened hands against her blouse. Her body was swept with a fire of intense longing. With a need so overwhelming that it consumed whatever fear or hesitancy lingered from her past. Matt deserved a woman who was as brave and courageous as he was being right now. Jenny understood the cost to him to admit what lay in his heart. More than anything, she believed him.

Lifting her chin, she met and drowned in his stormy gray gaze. Shivering with anticipation, she whispered unsteadily, "You're a man of honor, Matt. I know you mean it when you tell me you want me for all the right reasons." Lifting her hand, Jenny placed her palm against the side of his recently shaved face. There were so many small scars across his flesh. It hurt her to think how he'd received them. She knew there had to be some traumatic story behind each one, and that made her stomach clench in hurt.

When she touched him, his face grew tender... with love? What was she seeing in his eyes? Gulping, she couldn't be sure. Could he love her? Was she worth loving? Judging from his intent expression, the answer was an undeniable yes. She saw his strong lips part. His hands ranged upward from her shoulders to her face and framed it gently.

"I'll never be the warrior that you are, Matt."

"In my eyes, my heart, Jenny, you're already a heroine, a survivor, and I admire and respect the hell out of you for that. I don't care how you see yourself. What matters is how you really are. Do you understand that, darlin'?"

She closed her eyes and nodded slightly. His hands were so warm and comforting against her cheeks. "You deserve someone brave. Someone you can count on, Matt. You've helped me be stronger, and believe more in myself. You've been such a wonderful friend to me that I don't know where to begin—''

"Shh," he rasped, "don't tell me, Jenny. Show me how you feel about me. That's the place to start. We have a friendship. We respect and admire one another. Let's build on that. What do you say?'' He held his breath as he saw the effect his roughly spoken words had on her. The languid desire in Jenny's eyes as she opened them made him groan. Her lips were parted, and he saw the lower one tremble slightly as she boldly stepped forward, melted against him and placed her hands around his neck, drawing him downward...to kiss him.

Matt whispered her name like a prayer as he felt the first, tentative brush of her lips against his. A groan ripped from him. Instantly, he drew her close. She was soft, rounded, and seemed to flow against the harder angles of his tense body. Her arms wound around his neck and she stretched upward, her mouth opening to his hungry, searching lips. She tasted of sweet cinnamon and coffee. Her breathing came in chaotic bursts, warm and tingling against his sensitized flesh.

Inhaling deeply, Matt dragged in the gingery, womanly scent that was hers alone. Jenny was in his arms! She was kissing him! Wanting to reward her courage, her boldness, because he knew that she had to overcome a lot of fear to open herself up to him, Matt softened his mouth against hers. When he ran his tongue across her lower lip, a small moan trembled from her—a moan of pleasure. Satisfaction roared through him.

Desperately wanting to make her part of him, Matt ranged his hands across her slender arms and shoulders. He wanted to cup his fingers around her breasts, but stopped himself. This was a kiss of introduction, of mutual exploration, he sternly reminded himself. Yet his body was hard with need. Hot like fire itself, Matt was sure that Jenny was more than a little aware of his aroused state as her hips brushed naively against his.

Jenny drowned in the splendor of Matt's mouth. She hungrily drank from him. He was strong and sure, and shared that with her. It gave her the courage to boldly return his ardor. Her lower body throbbed with a smoldering fire that exploded violently to life as his mouth glided commandingly against her waiting lips.

Lost within the splintering sunlight and heat his mouth evoked, Jenny entrusted herself entirely to his strong, hard body. Matt's arms felt incredibly secure around her. Pressed against him as she was, she was wildly aware of his need of her. Intense, melting heat flowed through her like a river of lava. Never had a kiss spun her into a realm of such beauty and joy as this one was.

All too soon, he drew away. Jenny was confused. Her heart hammered violently in her chest as he reluctantly eased her away from him, his hands firm on her upper arms. Yet the predatory look in his silvery eyes sizzled through her, awakening her senses, and her mouth throbbed with the male power of him claiming her as his own.

"Your next interview is in ten minutes," he rasped. A deprecating smile pulled at one corner of his mouth as he reached out and tamed her hair back into place. "I think we need to get ourselves together for it, okay?"

Matt was right. With a slight moan, Jenny held on to his arm for a moment more. "Y-you're right...yes..." And she took a deep, shaky breath as she gazed up at him. "You kiss so wonderfully...."

Matt's returning grin was that of a peacock who was very pleased with himself, and she laughed breathlessly. She could still taste him on her lips. It was a heady discovery filled with promise.

"Me? A good kisser?"

"Yes, you," she declared. Finally, Jenny let go of him and stepped away. She didn't want to. She wanted to kiss Matt again and again, and explore him slowly. So slowly and deliciously, with her hands, her body, her lips. Matt was bringing out a decidedly sensual side of herself she'd never encountered before. Although surprising to Jenny, she reveled in it. "You make me feel intensely. I feel my body more than I ever have."

Her blush was demure and her honesty heart-wrenching to Matt. Sliding his hand along her jaw, he whispered, "You do the same thing to me, Jenny. I think there's a lot we have in common, don't you?"

"Oh, yes," she answered with a slight, embarrassed laugh. Moving awkwardly around the desk, she sat down before she fell down, her knees feeling suddenly mushy. Her mind and focus weren't on the coming interview at all. She opened the desk and pulled out her purse. After brushing her hair, she tried to pat her blouse back into place, and hoped she looked unmussed and presentable.

Matt sat on the edge of the desk, a predatory smile on his mouth and a gleam in his eyes that said *You're mine. All mine.*

It was late afternoon as they walked away from the helicopter pad and ambled down the dirt path parallel to the railroad tracks that would take them into Agua Caliente. This time Jenny slipped her hand into Matt's. He carried her briefcase in his other hand.

Jenny gave him a tender smile and Matt felt joy rise in his chest as never before. That one, perfect kiss had told her what lay in his heart. Matt knew he didn't have fancy words. Women often did a great job of communicating, but he felt like he had two left hands and a tongue to match when he tried to tell someone how he felt. His feelings for Jenny had been translated through that life-altering kiss he'd shared with her earlier.

As they walked along the path, Matt spotted bright yellow orchids with luscious red lips. One day, as Jenny had played in the shallow pool along the tributary, where all the children were safe from the strong, powerful currents, Maria had told Matt in a confidential voice about this flower. It was the marriage orchid, she'd whispered. She'd had a wicked glimmer in her chocolate-brown eyes as she looked pointedly downstream to where Jenny was crouched next to Daniel, playing with his dearly beloved red rubber ball. Maria confided conspiratorially to Matt that a man who was thinking of marrying the woman of his heart would always give her this orchid, for it was a symbol of his intent to ask her for her hand and heart, to be his wife someday soon. At the time, Matt had wondered if his feelings were that transparent. They must have been.

Leaning down now, he pulled Jenny gently to a halt. ''Hold on,'' he told her as he snapped off the round, green stem of the orchid. Straightening, he turned and put the briefcase down beside him. Placing the orchid stem in the top buttonhole of her blouse, he arranged it so that the blossom lay against her shoulder, just beneath her chin.

The orchid was fragrant, and Jenny closed her eyes and drew in a breath. "How beautiful," she whispered in awe, and reached out, sliding her hand down his forearm. Opening her eyes, she said, "Thank you, Matt...that's so sweet and thoughtful of you. I've never had a man give me flowers before."

He stared in shock at her comment, then swallowed his surprise. Picking up her briefcase, he turned and led her down a well-worn path to the tributary. "Well, expect them often from me."

Matt liked the daily schedule they'd fallen into. Jenny always saved her dessert from lunch at the base to bring back to Daniel. Maria was always down at the tributary this time of day, pounding the soapy clothes for her clients. Little Daniel, who always waited anxiously to spot them, would wave and jump up and down. He knew the dessert was coming.

Jenny touched the orchid. "It's beautiful, Matt. Thank you." He was so tender. So thoughtful. And yet to look at him, at that hard, warrior's face and mouth, no one would ever suspect he had such a romantic side to him. Jenny smiled. "This day is perfect, Matt. Perfect in every way."

As they made their way down the steep part of the path to the roaring tributary, he said, "The first day of the rest of our lives."

His meaning wasn't lost on Jenny. She saw the

burning desire in Matt's eyes as he turned and looked at her on the path, which was only wide enough for one person to traverse at a time. Long, hip-high grass grew luxuriantly on either side of the trail. The sun was shining brightly between powder-puff white clouds. The constant, throaty roar of the Urubamba filled the air around them.

Keeping a steadying grip on Jenny's hand, Matt led her to the shelf of rock where at least twenty Peruvian women toiled away with their laundry. Halfway down the bank, little Daniel, dressed in a bright red shirt and shabby, brown cotton trousers, his feet bare and muddy, waved gleefully toward them. Matt grinned as Jenny moved ahead of him, waving gaily back at the youngster. He saw Maria down on her hands and knees at her favorite flat rock on the edge of the churning water, the clothes wet and soapy as she beat them methodically with the smooth, gray stone in her hands. She looked up and nodded, giving them a wide, welcoming smile.

As they approached, Matt noted the long coil of white hemp rope near Maria. When she was finished washing the clothes, she'd string the hundred feet or so of rope from one spindly tree on the bank to another, and then hang the dripping garments there to dry overnight. In the morning, she'd come down and collect the clothes, fold them and carry them in baskets to her clients, who would give her a few soles for her efforts.

Maria's eyes danced as she saw Jenny approach. Her smile increased immensely and she called to her, commenting on the orchid she wore.

Matt realized Jenny didn't know what the orchid symbolized. That was all right. In time, he'd share that with her.

The bank of the tributary was mostly rock, and a little grainy sand. Daniel ran brokenly along the edge of the roaring tributary, on small, brown, spindly legs, his ball in his left hand. His eyes were wide and he was calling Jenny's name as he hopped and leaped over the gray, black and speckled boulders.

Matt stopped near Maria to say hello. Then he put the briefcase down and looked up in time to see a horrifying sight.

Daniel was hurrying across the rocky terrain toward Jenny when his muddy feet slipped on a smooth rock. The boy yelped and the red ball he carried in his hand flew out into the swirling water as he tried to regain his balance. Daniel turned and cried out, reaching for the ball, which bobbed only a few feet away in an eddy of icy water.

Matt started to shout. Maria shrieked and leaped to her feet, her cry echoing over the noise of the river. But it was too late. Her son vaulted into the river to retrieve his ball. In seconds, he was swept out into the wicked current.

Matt's voice was drowned out by the roar of the Urubamba as he saw Jenny drop the cake plate she carried. Without hesitation, without even thinking, she leaped into the water to try and grab Daniel's small, extended hand. Instead, the deadly undercurrent yanked her booted feet out from under her! In a split second she disappeared into the foaming blue-green water.

Chapter Eleven

The instant Jenny hit the water and felt her feet ripped from beneath her by the raging current, she screamed. It wasn't a scream of fear as much as it was a response to the icy coldness of the water, which sucked her breath out of her in a millisecond.

She heard Matt's voice above the roar, the absolute fear in it. There wasn't even time to look, for the current hurled her out into the frothing, twisting waves and into the path of a huge, ocher-colored boulder the size of a small car. To her horror, she saw little Daniel strike the side of it, bounce off and go under. Instinctively, because she couldn't fight the raging, angry current, Jenny drew her feet up close to her body, wrapped her arms around herself and took a deep breath of air before she struck the looming boulder full force.

Pain arced along the right side of Jenny's body. The violent flow dragged her beneath the water as she ricocheted off the rock. An unseen but deadly whirlpool hauled her under again.

No! Jenny kicked violently. Popping up to the surface with a gasp, she saw Daniel just ahead of her. He was shrieking and flailing awkwardly, his small mouth contorted. Fear made his eyes bulge. Jenny kicked outward and lunged for all she was worth, her hand stretched toward him.

Yes! Her whitened fingers wrapped strongly around Daniel's small wrist. As the tributary twisted her around and around, she hauled Daniel against her body with all her strength. The child stopped shrieking, his eyes pleading and anxious. His small arms clasped in a death grip around her neck.

Jenny went under. *No! Oh, no! Not like this!* She lunged hard and resurfaced. Trying to get oriented, she heard Matt's voice roaring above the river's thundering. Flinging her head to get the hair out of her eyes, Jenny saw him running parallel to them, fifty feet away. His face was set, his mouth a slash. In his hands he carried the hemp rope that Maria used to hang her clothes with. He was running hard, dodging the larger boulders, slipping and flailing as his booted feet hit the rocky, uneven surface of the bank. In an instant, Jenny realized what he was going to try and do. Wrenching around till she faced the upcoming opening in the Urubamba she realized there was less than a hundred yards to go before they were vomited into that relentless, unforgiving river.

Daniel's hand clawed in panic at her face. He was shrieking with terror. Jenny gripped him hard. She tried to pull his fingers away from her eyes so that she could see as the current spun them around once more.

Going under again because the icy temperature was sucking the heat and strength out of her body, she found water flooding violently up into her flared nostrils and opened mouth. Darkness closed around her as she struggled to push upward once more, to the surface. To life-giving air. Her boots, now waterlogged, were becoming deadly weights on her feet. They tugged her downward. There was no time, no way to get them off, for they were laced tightly. If she tried, she might lose Daniel, and she couldn't do that.

As she shot to the surface, she grabbed Daniel under the arms and held him high so that he wouldn't go under and drown. Everything was beginning to slow down. Jenny felt as if her life was a movie, being shot in sluggish, slow-motion frames. To her right, running hard and screaming, was Daniel's mother. Behind her, about ten or fifteen villagers were hot on her heels. All of them were trying to catch up to Matt, who was well ahead of them.

Daniel's sobbing screams of unrelenting terror tore through Jenny. The river ripped at her, once again contorting her sense of direction and twisting her around. Without warning, because she couldn't see it, she was smashed savagely into another boulder.

A cry ripped from her as she slammed into the obstacle. Again her right side took the brunt of the blow. Jenny felt something give way there and pain arced up into her chest. She shrieked in agony, but her hands tightened around Daniel as she continued to try and hold him up out of the grasping, greedy water churning and bubbling around them.

Again, as she bounced off the side of another boulder, the undertow around it hauled her down. Down, down, down. She felt Daniel struggling. He was below the surface. Water tunneled up into her nose as she fought the deadly whirlpool. They would both die if she didn't fight back!

The thought of Daniel dying was too much for Jenny to accept. From somewhere deep within her, she found strength. Adrenaline streaking through her body, she kicked. Kicked savagely. Kicked upward. Air! Oh, God, they had to have air!

Jenny shot up and out of the water with a cry. As she vomited violently, water regurgitating from her lungs and up through her mouth and nose, she heard Daniel whimper. His clinging grasp on her neck was weaker. She saw the fear in his dark brown eyes. He was gasping for air and choking.

Fifty yards to go.

Using the last of her strength, Jenny righted herself so that she was facing the Urubamba, which seemed to be rushing to them. On the edge of the bank where the tributary met the river, she saw Matt skid to a halt, mud flying around him. She saw the terror in his eyes as he began to make a loop on the end of the rope. And then he gathered it up in his large hands and began to twirl the loop around and around his head like a cowboy getting ready to rope a steer.

Her mind was groggy now, the cold water making her hypothermic to the point where she couldn't think clearly. Yet Jenny sluggishly realized what he was going to try and do. He was going to throw the loop out to them. If she could catch it in time, Matt could haul them to safety before they were carried into the Urubamba River.

Jenny knew she was dead. She knew it in her heart, in her soul. Yet she also knew Daniel had to live! If only she could catch that rope Matt was going to throw! He would have only one chance. *One.* For if they were swept into the Urubamba, they would both die. The current was unforgiving, swift and deadly.

Her heart rebelled. She couldn't die! Daniel couldn't drown! He was too young! He had his entire life in front of him! As Jenny was spun around again, slammed into another boulder, she realized something else. Something so precious, so life-giving, that it created an inner fire of determination that she'd never experienced before in her life. She loved Matt Davis. Unequivocally. Forever. And dammit, she wanted a chance to pursue that love with him!

Like a race horse floundering toward the finish line despite the fact that he had absolutely no strength left, Jenny resolved not to quit no matter what. Her determination, her desire to live, exploded through her like a nuclear bomb detonating within her heart and soul.

In those seconds that crawled by, Jenny gritted her teeth. She kicked hard and fought the sucking, grasping current. Her strength was gone. She could feel her life being stolen by the icy water, the cold sucking it out of her like a greedy vampire. *No! No, I won't go down without a fight! I won't! I love you, Matt! Oh, I love you! Please…please, give me the strength, help me! I want to tell you that! Oh, please, help me!*

As she popped up to the surface, her feet pointed downstream, she heard Matt hoarsely calling her. Instantly, she lifted her hand high, preparing to try and catch the rope that was swinging above his head. The relief in his eyes was momentous as he saw that she understood what he was going to try to do. There was no way, even though he was a SEAL, that he could just jump in and rescue her, Jenny knew. No one could beat this river, with its deadly currents and icy temperature.

For an instant, Jenny bobbed on the surface of a quiet place between two huge boulders. She kept her hand held high, her numb, white fingers stretched outward like claws.

It was then that Matt threw the loop. He'd seen that quiet space between the boulders and had prayed that the current would carry Jenny and Daniel into it. It was the only smooth water in the whole tributary. His aim had to be precise. If the rope landed too far in front of them, it would be whisked away instantly by the current. If it landed too far behind, Jenny would be unable to swim upstream to try and reach it.

He saw how white her face was. He knew she was suffering from deep hypothermia. No one knew better than Matt what hypothermia could do to a body. It robbed victims of their mind, their ability to think. They became confused. Disoriented. Worst of all, the icy water sucked the life out of a person. First it stole the heat out of the muscles, then the muscles slowed down. Finally, they stopped working, because the cold literally froze them in place. And that was when a person drowned.

He saw Jenny's distorted mouth, the cry on her pale, bluish lips. Little Daniel was clinging to her neck in a death grip. Matt was sure she wasn't getting adequate air. And judging from the amount of water she was swallowing, it was only a matter of time before she'd run out of oxygen and slip quietly, forever, beneath the waves of the violent, angry water.

One chance. He had one chance. His heart thundered in his chest as he saw that her hand was still raised upward. *Yes!* She was still coherent. Still able to think. Maria and the rest of the villagers gathered around him, panicked and anxious. They halted, panting, and clasped their hands together in prayer. He swung the loop high above his head, steadying it as best he could. One chance...

More than anything, Matt realized he loved Jenny in that moment. And his anger and need of her were heightened knowing there was a good chance she would drown with Daniel and be swept away by the Urubamba. Anguish seared his chest, and it felt like a branding iron was burning his heart. He'd just found her! He'd just realized how wonderful she was. And he needed her. More than any person in his life, he needed her.

Hand tightening on the rope coils in his left hand, he timed his throw. The moment Jenny drifted between those boulders and the water smoothed, he sent the loop snaking out powerfully toward her raised hand.

Everyone held their breath.

Someone cried out.

Jenny's hand was up, her fingers grasping toward the sky, her flesh white, her fingertips blue. She saw the loop skittering in their direction. The current turned her sideways. No! Fighting the exhaustion, fighting the weariness that was seeping rapidly through her body now, she forced herself around.

She twisted back just in time to have the rope strike her clawing fingers. Yes! The loop settled over Daniel—*good!* She was so tired. The current started to pull her away from the eddy and out into the frothing, bubbling waters. *Get the rope around herself!* Her mind kept screaming at her to do it, over and over again. But her hand wouldn't obey her mind. The loop was around Daniel. She tried to pick it up and drag it across her wet head, but the hemp tumbled out of her nerveless grasp. She had seconds to go before they'd be swept into the Urubamba.

At least Daniel could be saved—that was what her mind told her. Jenny fumbled again with the loop, her fingers numb. She could feel nothing. With her other arm, she held Daniel protectively against her. The loop dropped again. With a weak cry, Jenny felt a huge, tugging sensation. A powerful current snarled around her legs as she wearily continued to kick to keep them afloat.

Looking to her left, she realized they were now being sucked into the Urubamba itself. Crying out, her lips contorted, she closed her eyes. This was it. She was going to die. At least Daniel would live....

But then, as they made the turn and began to flow into the Urubamba, Jenny opened her eyes. A resolve, deep and surprising, flashed through her. In that moment when everything seemed to be moving with such anguished and excruciating slowness, she picked up the loop one last time. She forced her fingers to close around the rope, though she couldn't feel the soggy line.

Matt was roaring at her. His voice was drowned out by the thundering Urubamba as they were swept out into it.

A bolt of energy flashed through her. Jenny felt it crackling and moving like hot, boiling lava down her arms and into her frozen, unresponsive fingers. That surge of heat gave her the strength to pull the loop up and across her head. The rope slipped around her shoulders, with Daniel within it as well.

Matt cried out. He needed help! Instantly, several village men came down the hill and were on that rope behind him. He jerked it taut and saw the loop tighten instantly around Jenny and Daniel. They were being swept out into the mighty river so fast that it boggled his mind.

The moment the rope grew taut, Matt hauled back on it with all his weight. Jenny and Daniel were drifting out toward a massive set of boulders. If they struck them, they would be knocked unconscious by the fury and speed of the current. Five men hauled back with him at the same time. Grunts and groans broke out. He watched, his breath snagging in his chest, as they fought against the current. Two lives dangled on the end of that line. What if the rope broke? How strong was it? He didn't know. His lips curled away from his clenched teeth.

"Pull!" he cried out in Spanish. *"Pull hard!"*

The villagers grunted and groaned again. Backs bent. Feet dug into the muddy bank, then slipped. Fingers groped savagely as the escaping rope sizzled through their hands. *Stop it! Stop the rope from escaping!*

Matt dug the heels of his boots into the rock and mud, and leaned backward with his full weight. The rope pulled taut! They'd stopped it from escaping. He watched helplessly as Jenny went under with Daniel in her arms. *No!* He knew why she had gone under. He knew this would happen.

"Faster. Faster!" he screamed at the others.

Every man was pulling as hard as he could on that rope to try and bring them to shore. But as the villagers pulled, Jenny and Daniel were dragged underwater. The very act of rescuing them could kill them now.

Tears of rage and frustration stung Matt's eyes. He saw the current raging over Jenny's blond, limp hair. He saw her holding Daniel's head above the water the best she could, even though she was beneath the suffocating flow herself. Tears washed into the sides of his contorted mouth. He could taste the salt of them. His eyes were narrowed to slits. His heart pounded frantically in his chest.

There! Jenny's head bobbed to the surface as they finally hauled them closer to shore. They dragged her nearer, up across the hidden boulders and rocks at the river's edge. He saw her hands fall away from Daniel. She was unconscious. He knew she'd taken in a lot of water. Luckily, the rope kept Daniel against her as they hauled them the last ten feet to safety.

When they were close enough to shore, Matt dropped the rope and lunged forward. The bank was steep. He skidded down the rocky slope toward where Jenny lay on her side, unconscious, half out of the water. Daniel was screaming. He was flailing and trying to keep his face out of the water.

The men of the village were on Matt's heels. They tumbled and leaped to get to them, as well.

Matt reached them first. He splashed out into the knee-deep water, slipping and sliding on the algae-covered rocks. He nearly lost his footing. With one hand, he gripped Daniel by the scruff of his shirt. With the other, he grabbed Jenny beneath her right arm. Lifting their dead weight, he fell backward with both of them in his arms.

As he hit the shallow water, Matt bruised himself against the rocks. One of the villagers—Daniel's father, Juan—reached him and grabbed his sobbing son from Matt's grasp. The child was swung upward, passed to another man closer to shore, and then lifted by a sea of outstretched hands to the safety of the bank and his mother's open arms.

Matt felt strong, supportive hands sliding beneath his armpits. Two men dragged him upright as he held on to Jenny. She was unconscious. Her face was bluish colored. Her once-beautiful, sun-colored hair lay limp and clinging to the icy flesh of her face.

Once on shore, Matt managed to stand with the help of the men who protectively surrounded him. In one ragged motion, he lifted Jenny against him and turned. The villagers realized he had to give her artificial respiration, but couldn't do it on this rocky slope. He had to have a smooth, uncluttered area where he could lay her out and work on her. Without a word, they turned and helped him struggle up the rocky, slippery bank to the red clay bank above.

Gasping and panting, Matt laid Jenny down on her belly. He quickly pulled her arms above her head and straightened out her small, precious body. Turning her face to one side, he quickly straddled her. With his hands, he pushed on the middle of her back in a forward motion toward her shoulders. The villagers crowded around in a circle. Many prayed out loud. Others watched, their eyes huge, their mouths open in silent distress.

With the first savage effort, water came gurgling out of Jenny's slack, parted lips. Again Matt pushed. More water. He growled her name.

"Jenny! Come back to me! Dammit, don't you die on me. Not now! Not like this!"

He pushed again. More water.

How much had she swallowed? The little fool! She'd gone under to keep Daniel above the waves. She'd knowingly given her life for his. Tears stung Matt's slitted eyes as he worked feverishly over her. Pumping the water out of her didn't guarantee anything. When no more came out, he quickly got off her and rolled her over. Jenny was like a limp, wet rag doll.

As he leaned over her, his ear near her nostrils and slack mouth, he could feel no breath. Jenny wasn't breathing! He felt for her pulse with shaking fingers. *Nothing.* She was dead.

"No!" he howled. *No!* Not like this!

Leaning down, Matt eased her head back, propped her chin up and cupped it with his shaking hands. He pinched her nostrils closed with his fingers and settled his mouth firmly against her lips. He was alarmed at how cold she was. It was then that Matt realized the courage she'd had to stay coherent, to stay conscious that long. Not even a SEAL could have survived that river and that temperature without a wet suit, and Jenny had. She'd survived long enough to know that Daniel would live.

Pumping two breaths into her, Matt watched her chest rise beneath the wet, clinging material across her breasts. Then he straddled her again and put his hand on her sternum, pumping it five times, hard and solid, to shock the heart into starting. He heard a *crack*. He knew he'd just broken her sternum with the force of his hands, but it was unavoidable. He *had* to save her!

Again he breathed his breath into her. Again he shocked her heart. She had to come back to him! She had to!

Grayness began to replace the darkness that Jenny found herself floating within. She saw a tunnel of light and recognized people she had loved, who had died, standing in the middle of it. And then she saw two white figures. They were indistinct, and yet the sense of love that emanated from them was overwhelming as they floated toward her in that glowing tunnel.

Go back.

She stood there, confused by their telepathic order. The figures, which towered over her now, were luminous and filmy-looking as they spoke to her once more.

Go back. Your time is not yet. You must return.

The moment those words echoed through her

mind, Jenny felt herself being sucked downward into what felt like a swiftly moving, circular tornado of energy. As she was whirling and spinning downward, the light dimmed and grew black…and then…colors. She was seeing rainbow colors…. Her lids moved. She felt heat. She heard gasping. She heard people talking in low, stressed voices. What was going on?

Her lids fluttered. Jenny felt warm, strong hands lifting her upward. Her head lolled against someone's shoulder. And then she felt the first stab of pain in her right side and in the center of her chest.

It was the pain that brought her to consciousness. Yet as she came to, she felt as if she were being cradled in loving arms. She felt the trembling touch of someone's fingertips across her brow, felt them brush her hair from her eyes and cheek. What had happened?

After a struggle, Jenny finally opened her eyes. The first thing she saw was Matt leaning over her, his eyes wide with fear and anxiety. He was holding her in his arms. And Jenny saw another emotion in his narrowed gray eyes: love. Love for her. It was the oddest moment of her life, as she felt strung between that tunnel of light and here, back in her body. She could read his mind, feel what was in his heart. It was the most astounding revelation to her, for she'd never experienced telepathy before.

Jenny clung to his stormy looking gaze and felt

his arms tighten protectively around her. How safe she felt! And when she dragged her lids open even more, she saw the tension in the slash of his mouth ease. She saw his lips part. And then she heard words she never thought she'd ever hear from him.

"Jenny? Jenny, are you all right? It's Matt." His voice cracked. Tears flooded his eyes as he continued to caress her damp hair with his trembling hand. "I love you. Do you hear me? I love you. Don't you leave. Don't you ever leave! You hear me?"

Chapter Twelve

"Are you warm now?" Matt whispered against the damp hair near Jenny's ear. He was lying on their bed, his back against the headboard. She was tucked in a thick, warm alpaca blanket, her head resting tiredly against his chest. A soft sigh broke from her, and he squeezed her gently because she'd suffered a set of very badly bruised ribs. The doctor who had examined her had said that the cartilage portion of the sternum was cracked, as well. That would heal up in about three weeks. The ribs would take as long, or maybe a little longer.

Closing her eyes, Jenny whispered, "Yes, I feel *much* better." The last two hours had been the most horrifying and the most joyous of her life. Never had Jenny experienced such care and tenderness from a man. She'd barely been conscious when Matt had hoisted her up in his arms after she had nearly died. So many other hands—of village women who passed alpaca blankets to her to keep her warm. Village men who helped Matt—had touched her as well.

Nearly half the village had followed Matt as he walked quickly to the plaza and into the small medical clinic. Right behind him were Daniel and his parents. Jenny was worried for Daniel, but compared to her the little boy seemed unharmed by his brush with death.

She couldn't stop crying as the doctor examined her behind the cloth curtain. Luckily, Matt never left her side, never allowed his hand to slip from her shaking shoulders. Since she had been nearly hypothermic, Matt had stripped her out of her wet clothing, nearly tearing off her boots and heavy socks. He'd wrapped her tightly in several blankets and then sat her up on the gurney and begun to briskly rub her back, shoulders and arms to force the blood to flow.

The nurse had given her coca leaf tea to drink, because it was warm. But most of all, Matt's care had brought her back to life. Now Jenny wondered if she'd heard things as she lay on the bank near death. Had Matt really said he loved her? Her heart contracted. Snuggling beneath his hard, unforgiving jaw, she tucked her bruised hand beneath her chin and felt the lull of exhaustion creeping over her. Just the way his hand trembled lightly on her drying hair made her want to start crying all over again.

Matt closed his eyes and held her gently. "You almost died out there today," he said in a low, rasping tone against her ear. "Jenny...I was so scared. Scared of losing you." Compressing his lips, his brow wrinkling, Matt knew he had to get out how he felt toward her. Would Jenny push him away? Was his love one-sided? Would she become scared and run? He had no way of knowing, but in his gut he sensed that Jenny was far stronger and more resilient than he'd ever given her credit for. Anyone who would leap into that icy coffin called a river to save another's life was heroic beyond his scope of understanding. She was a real-life heroine. And she had a heart as huge as the universe. More than anything, he wanted to share his own heart with her. Would she feel the same way?

Matt felt her stir at his murmured admission. He eased her back just enough so that her head rested on his shoulder and she could look up at him. Her eyes swam with tears, but the flecks of golden sunlight in their depths gave him the courage to go on. His hands tightened slightly on her shoulder and the hand he held. Such a small, delicate hand. But what a courageous heart she had. Giving her a slight, unsteady smile, he added, "Did you hear me out there earlier? You may not have. You were going down for the count. Maybe you weren't conscious enough…."

Jenny felt her heart began to skip beats. She saw the stormy, narrowed look in Matt's eyes and knew…knew what he was going to say. Her heart expanding like a flower opening, she held her breath and waited.

"Hell…Jenny, I love you." There, it was out on the table. Now she could either accept or reject him. Matt felt suffocated in those seconds as he saw his words register. Her eyes widened enormously. Her petal-perfect lips parted. There was shock and…something else in her eyes. What it was, Matt wasn't sure.

Matt's strained features blurred. Since becoming conscious, all Jenny could do was weep off and on, having no control over her ragged, tattered emotional state. Huge tears formed and rolled down her cheeks as she held his anxious gaze.

"Y-you do?"

Licking his lips, Matt growled, "Yes. How do you feel about me?" His heart bounded once. Hard. Never had he been so scared as now—and he was an ex-Navy SEAL, who had encountered hundreds of situations where he'd been scared to death. But not like this. Her tears tore at him. He lifted his hand from her smaller cooler one and tenderly wiped her tears away with his callused fingers.

Choking on words that stuck in her throat, Jenny closed her eyes as his gentle touch caressed not only her flesh, but her aching heart, and made it expand with euphoria. As he drew his hand away, she caught it, her still-white fingers wrapping around his thicker, stronger ones. "I can't explain it, Matt," Jenny began brokenly. Gripping his hand, she confessed, "I feel like such a coward. You've got more courage than I do. I—I've been feeling so strongly toward you since I met you that it's been driving me crazy. I was afraid to call it love because it seemed too soon. I was scared...that maybe how I felt about you wasn't how you might feel toward me." Gulping unsteadily, she could barely hold his burning gaze. "Does that make sense?"

Whispering her name, Matt carefully turned Jenny so that she was facing him fully. Cognizant of her bruised ribs, he maneuvered her so that her drawn-up legs settled against his hip. With one arm around her blanketed shoulders, he released her hand and cupped her face.

"Do you know how priceless you are to me, sweet woman? How I look forward to waking up with you beside me every morning? I've been fighting myself every night not to drag you into my arms and love you until your body sang with joy along with mine. So many times your melodic laughter had flowed through me and lifted me up. You make me feel happier than I've ever deserved to be.''

Sighing audibly, Jenny closed her eyes. "You're so beautiful with your words, Matt...a poet." Touching her heart with her hand, she reopened her eyes and stared warmly up into his. "I think I've loved you from the beginning."

Nodding, Matt felt an avalanche of fear melting off his tense shoulders. Jenny loved him! Heart soaring, he tried to keep it in perspective. Grazing her cheek, which was now damp with tears and rosy with emotion, he said, "I think I did, too. I think it took this incident to drive it home—to both of us."

Nodding, Jenny closed her eyes and absorbed his continuing touch. "Yes...yes, it did...." As he caressed her, his fingers created a pleasant, building fire from her temple and cheek, down to her neck. In that moment, she felt like a sacred vessel—much loved, hotly desired.

Swallowing hard, Matt kept his caress light and tender. He saw the pleasure in Jenny's sweet face and smiled inwardly as her lips parted. He continued to explore her face, neck and small, proud shoulders, but he told himself not to go too far. She was in no condition to make love. Bruised ribs were as bad as broken ones, as far as he was concerned. She couldn't even take in a full breath of air because of the pain. Luckily, the bruises were low on her rib cage, and she was able to wear a tight spandex wrap to keep them protected and stable. No, right now, all he wanted to do was let her know how much he loved her. Touch was one form of communication, one he was very good at. And Jenny needed to be cradled, cared for, nourished and held as never before. After all, she had died back there on the banks of the Urubamba. She had told him earlier about the tunnel of light and how she was told to go back, that it wasn't her time yet. When he'd heard that, fear shot through him like an icy pick stabbing him through his thudding heart. His breath had brought her back. Back to him. Now everything else could wait. They had time now. Precious time.

"Kiss me, Matt?"

Her voice was trembling. He saw her lovely blue eyes open. Saw the tears, the joy, the shining light in her gaze that was meant only for him. This time, he realized her tears were happy ones. To be shared. Giving her a very male smile, he cupped Jenny's face with his hands and leaned down. Above all, he wanted her to know that he worshipped her. That she was priceless, and beyond anything he'd ever imagined for himself. Matt had thought love was a four-letter word that could only wound and hurt. Well, he was wrong. The woman whose lips he now grazed, whose breath he inhaled deeply into his heart, his needy soul, had shown him he was wrong.

A little moan moved through Jenny as Matt's strong, sure mouth covered her lips in a butterfly light caress. His hands were steadying as she leaned upward, wanting more, desiring much more from him. Seeming to understand what she was asking, he pressed his lips firmly against hers, rocking hers open and moving his tongue languidly against her own. The effect was so surprising, so potent, that Jenny quivered.

"Like that?" Matt whispered raggedly against her ear. He opened his eyes and saw her grow languid beneath his stroking caress. Something told him Jenny was not all that experienced in lovemaking, and until he knew for sure, he was going to take his time with her. He would teach her, share with her, find out what she liked and what she was ready for.

"Umm…" Jenny melted completely beneath the heated onslaught of his very male mouth. Just the brush of his bearded face against her cheek created wild tingles within her. Jenny lost herself in his strength, in his tender assault upon her senses. She felt him holding back, as if she would break if he was too rough with her. Under the circumstances, her reeling mind told her, she was in no condition to make love to him right now. Not with her cracked sternum and bruised ribs. Matt had more sense, more control than she did presently.

Gradually, Matt eased his mouth from hers. As he opened his eyes, his hands still framing her rosy cheeks, he saw the slumberous quality of Jenny's gaze as she peered wonderingly up at him. His lips curved ruefully. Moving his fingers across her unmarred brow, trailing them down the sides of her clean jaw, he whispered, "I love you, Jenny Wright. And I'm looking forward to the day when I can love you totally...."

She trembled at his husky tone and the caress of his fingers against her face and neck. Her breasts ached to be touched. The throbbing fire in her lower body was almost painful. Hungering for him desperately, she managed a soft, strained laugh as his hands settled back on her shoulders and he eased her around so that once again she lay against his warm bulk.

"I don't know if I can last that long," she murmured shyly. No man had ever looked at her and made her feel so feminine, so wanton, as the way Matt did. For whatever reason, he made her feel bold—deliciously so. At her comment, she saw that wonderful mouth of his crook in a kind of little-boy smile that melted her soul.

"Yeah?"

"Yeah," Jenny replied, grinning and putting a frisky note in her voice.

Laughing deeply, Matt hugged her, but carefully. He kissed her brow, her nose and dipped quickly down to capture her smiling mouth. "You know what, sweet woman? I think I've got a bead on you now. You go around with this meek, mild, shadowy facade.'' He tapped her nose teasingly. ''And you're really Princess Xena underneath—courageous, strong and invincible.''

Giggling, Jenny caught his hand. She basked in his tender teasing. ''Invincible? Oh, I think not. If you hadn't had the presence of mind to pick up that rope and toss it to me, I'd be dead now. No, I'm not invincible, darling…but with you, I feel that way. You're such a role model for me.''

Losing his smile, Matt cupped her chin. ''Listen to me, Jenny. Don't you ever think you aren't heroic, because you are. I'm a trained SEAL, and I'm not sure I would have survived that river. That water would freeze the strongest SEAL in minutes.'' Matt gave her a grave look. ''You were in that ice water for nearly three minutes, Jenny. Plenty long enough to go completely hypothermic, and you didn't. You held Daniel up above you so he wouldn't take in water until the very end. By that time, we had you in the shallows. You are so strong. You're passionate. It was that huge heart of yours that gave you the courage, the physical strength and doggedness to save that little boy.''

His words fed her. Nourished her starving soul as nothing else ever could. Matt was completely sincere in his analysis of her attributes, and he honored her decision to jump in after Daniel in spite of the danger. Suddenly she saw herself in a way she never had before. Sliding her fingertips across his raspy face, Jenny whispered, "Your belief in me, that I could be courageous…a heroine…helped me believe in myself. Believe that I could do what I did." She gazed up at him, knowing he was her role model. "Isn't that what love is really all about, Matt? One partner supports and helps the other become all that they can be? Love means building up, not tearing down."

Nodding, he rasped, "Yes. Yes, it is, Jenny." Catching her hand, Matt pressed a warm, long kiss to the center of her palm and watched her eyes grow slumberous with pleasure again. "I think a couple of days of rest are what you need now. I'm going to talk to Major Stevenson, ask her for some time off to let you heal up before we finish these interviews. Okay?"

Her brows shot up. Jenny sat up, too quickly. She grimaced and tenderly held her ribs with her hand. "No! No…don't do that! I promised her I wouldn't take up a lot of her time. She simply doesn't have it. I'm fine, Matt. I want to go to the base tomorrow morning just as planned."

"Okay, tiger woman," he sighed. Giving her a charged look filled with love, he said, "You stay here. I'm going to go down to the plaza for a minute."

As he eased away and stood up, Jenny frowned. "Why?"

"Kannie and Patrick, owners of the India Feliz,

are making you your favorite meal, and they're walking it down here for you. It's their way of honoring and thanking you for saving little Daniel." He grinned. "And it's supposed to be a surprise, nosy."

She smiled softly. "That's so nice of them! They didn't have to do that."

Matt opened the door to their room and smiled back at her. "Expect to get a few accolades over your rescue, sweet woman. Well deserved, I'd say. I'll be right back."

Jenny was stunned when the civilian helicopter, flown by one of the Apache pilots masquerading as a civilian, flew them into the military side of the base instead of to the mining side, which was general protocol. She gripped the seat, her knuckles whitening, as Chief Warrant Officer Akiva Redtail whipped the small Bell helicopter through an opening in the black lava wall that led to the military complex. Jenny sucked in a sharp breath as Akiva moved the chopper through the hole, barely large enough to accommodate the whirling blades, as if she were on a Sunday drive. One wrong move, and Jenny saw all too clearly that the blades could smash into that unrelenting black basalt and they'd die in a fiery inferno. She felt Matt's hand settle over hers for reassurance.

No sooner had they cleared the hole than Akiva

said cheerfully over the intercom, "We call it the Eye. Extreme, eh?"

"Uh, yes…extreme…." Jenny whispered, fear lumped in her throat. She heard Akiva laugh huskily as she adroitly guided the helicopter to the lip, a smooth basalt slab at the edge of the gargantuan cave.

"Why are we landing on the military side?" she asked Akiva, frowning. They always flew to the mining side, their cover. And flying the Eye was a frightening experience for Jenny. Something she never wanted to do again.

Akiva maneuvered the Bell helicopter around, hovered and then descended to the deck of the cave. "Major Stevenson ordered me to bring you in this way," she told her enigmatically. She lowered the helicopter to the lip, settling gently on it. Immediately, Akiva cut the power and the blades began to slow. She turned and grinned at Jenny. "Take a look out there." And she pointed inside the cave.

They had to wait until the blades stopped turning before the ground crew could forward to place chalks beneath the tires of the helo and put the blades in a sling that would stop them from turning in the breeze.

From the grin on Matt's face, Jenny knew something was up. But what? Frowning, she leaned down and looked out the window toward the cave. Just about every single person who worked at the base was standing at stiff attention, in a rectangular formation. Everyone was in dark green, U.S. Army dress uniforms, not their normal workday clothing. She saw Majors Stevenson and York at the front of the ranks looking toward them expectedly, smiles of welcome on their faces.

"What's going on?" Jenny asked as Matt opened the door once the blades had stopped.

"A formation," Matt told her. He helped her out of the helicopter, taking care to lower her gently to the basalt floor so she wouldn't jar her taped ribs. Today, despite a little shyness on her part, Matt had helped Jenny to dress, because she couldn't raise her right arm far due to her painful ribs. He'd pulled out an apple-green blouse and khaki slacks for her this morning. She'd managed to wriggle into everything by herself, except she couldn't button the blouse. Matt tried not to make her feel embarrassed when he saw that she wore a simple white cotton chemise and not a bra beneath the blouse. Jenny had blushed furiously as he awkwardly fumbled to close all the buttons on the shirt, plus work the snap closed on her slacks. It was obvious Jenny didn't like feeling helpless.

Now she stared at the military formation, mystified. Akiva came around the helo, grinning like a jaguar who had sighted her quarry. Her cinnamon eyes shone with happiness. She looked over at Matt.

"Ready?"

Matt nodded and smiled down at Jenny, who was completely perplexed as to what was going on. She was not familiar with military procedures or protocol. As he slid his fingers beneath her left elbow and guided her toward the others, she hung back a little in trepidation.

"It's okay," he whispered as he leaned down, his lips near her ear. "This is for you, Jenny. It's a celebration of sorts."

Reluctantly, she fell into step with Matt. As they approached, the two commanding officers of the base came to attention and saluted her crisply. Confused, Jenny saw Akiva also come to attention and snap off a smart salute to her, as well.

"What's going on?" she asked Maya.

The CO smiled a little. To her left stood a woman at attention who was holding two items in her hands.

"Jenny? Why don't you come forward? We want to honor you."

Honor her? Why? Her head swam with even more confusion as Matt gently eased her forward so that she stood between Maya and ranks of uniformed personnel. Matt had a proud look on his face, his teeth even and white as he smiled at her.

"Jenny Wright?" Maya Stevenson's husky voice rang throughout the cavern.

Startled by her name being called so loudly, she gasped. And then Jenny gathered herself. Maya picked up an official-looking piece of paper and stepped smartly in her direction. Stopping in front of her, she faced the formation and began to read from it.

"Let it be known that civilian Jenny Wright is being honored for her bravery in saving the life of a little boy yesterday at the tributary in Aqua Caliente." Maya lifted her chin and nailed Jenny with a narrowed look. "As commanding officer of the Black Jaguar Squadron, it gives me great pleasure to award you the Purple Heart Medal, a medal reserved for someone wounded in action who turns and helps her comrades instead of thinking solely of herself."

Stunned, Jenny watched openmouthed as the brunette sergeant stepped up, carrying a small, gold velvet pillow that had a purple heart with a purple-and-white ribbon draped over it. Maya picked up the medal, and turning, moved briskly over to Jenny. Gently, Maya pinned the medal on the left side of her blouse. Stepping back, she saluted her, as did the other officers who stood nearby.

"At ease," Maya ordered her squadron.

Immediately, everyone relaxed and placed their hands behind their backs, alert to what their CO was going to say.

Jenny felt embarrassed. Maya had a slight smile playing across her full lips. The power this woman had was immense, and Jenny felt benign warmth flowing from her. Maya's emerald-green eyes softened. Her voice lowered a bit, but it still rang clearly and strongly throughout the cavern, so that everyone present could hear her speak.

"Jenny, we like to honor anyone who places their own life secondarily to saving another. That's what this squadron is all about. Our lives are the line for the betterment of the world in general. When I was informed of your courageous act of bravery yesterday, I told my officers about it. We felt, to a person, that you should not only be publicly honored for what you did—and nearly died doing—but also given a military medal for your heroism."

Maya smiled a little and pointed to the medal. "We don't have civilian medals, but we wanted you to have one of ours so that you knew how much we honored your bravery. This medal happens to be one of too many that I have of this type...."

Polite laughter rippled through the formation. Jenny turned and looked at the smiling faces of the women squadron and the glimmer in their eyes as they looked at their CO. Clearly, Maya's leadership here was unquestioned, and her people loved and respected her.

Maya continued in a warm tone, "You suffered many wounds and nearly died rescuing that little boy. In our eyes and hearts, you are brave and heroic. We want you to keep this medal, the Purple Heart, as a token of our appreciation, esteem and respect for who and what you are. We're proud to have you as one of our own.''

Maya held out her hand to Jenny, smiling hugely.

In shock, Jenny looked over at Matt, who stood off to one side with Akiva. Jenny brought up her hand and shook Maya's. The CO's grip was like a steel trap. ''Th-thank you, Major Stevenson....'' And she released Maya's hand. Turning, she lifted her hand, a small smile on her lips. ''Thank you, everyone. This is so...so unexpected. I really don't know what to say....'' And she turned back to Maya, who was smiling over at her husband, Dane York.

They were honoring her! Jenny realized. They were celebrating her act of bravery in rescuing little Daniel. A lump formed in her throat. Everything blurred. Automatically, Jenny's badly bruised and cut hand went to the medal that hung on her blouse. Maya was giving her one of her own medals. A medal given for being wounded while in action and under fire. She smiled bravely through her tears at the tall woman warrior.

''I'm honored that it came from you and your squadron. I'll never forget this, Major. Not ever. Thanks so much. I never expected this....''

With a brisk nod, Maya lost her smile. She came up and handed Jenny a small piece of cloth. ''When someone in a squadron gives a person the squadron patch, it's like saying they're family. They're one of us.'' Pressing the round patch, which had a head of a snarling black jaguar on it, encircled with red and blue rings, into Jenny's palm, Maya added, ''Welcome to the base, Ms. Wright. You're now one of us, a black jaguar.''

Jenny's gaze clung to the patch, until the emblem blurred. Sniffing, she blinked through her tears. Matt approached and slid a tissue into her hand. She thanked him and wiped her eyes and blew her nose.

''This is all so wonderful,'' she said, strengthening her voice so the formation of smiling, nodding women could hear her. Lifting up the patch, Jenny said, ''I know none of you know me, but for so long, I never belonged to anyone, anywhere. I was a foster child. I don't want you to feel sorry for me. What I want you to know is how great it feels to finally be a recognized member of a larger family.''

There was instantaneous clapping and cheering. Some of the women whistled. Others cried out her name. Some smiled. And some had tears in their eyes.

Jenny turned and looked up at Maya, who had a tender look on her face. She could look very stern and official at times, but now Jenny could see deep emotion in her eyes, and in the smile lurking at the corners of her well-shaped mouth.

''I feel like you know what you've just given me.''

Nodding, Maya whispered, ''I do, Jenny. Now

you have a home. And we're all your sisters and brothers. From now on, you have a family. A big one.'' She gazed over at Matt, and stepped aside so that he could join them.

Jenny showed him the patch that lay in her palm. She saw the pride and love shining in his eyes for her. The applause continued. It was overwhelming to her. Wonderful. Unexpected. Exhilarating. As Matt put his arm tenderly around her shoulders and embraced her carefully, Jenny heard cries, yells, Indian war whoops from Akiva and wolf whistles from the men in the group. Matt kissed her lightly on the mouth and then eased away.

As he did, he rasped, ''Soak it all in, Jenny. You deserve this. They're honoring you because you are a real, live, honest-to-God heroine. I love you so much. You've got a heart as big and wide as the state of Montana.''

It was all too much for Jenny. After nearly dying yesterday afternoon, and then to have this raucous, sincere celebration in her honor, she couldn't stop the tears that trickled from her eyes. Oh, she knew she probably shouldn't show her tears in front of all these military people. But as she self-consciously wiped them away, she saw many of the squadron wiping moisture from their eyes, too.

No longer would she ever consider herself a coward. And she swore to never call herself a 'fraidy cat again. Her spirit lifted and then spread its wings and flew. Matt's arm around her shoulders was like sunlight to Jenny. The look of pride mixed with love in his expression was all she would ever need. Now, she could come to his side a whole person, not a frightened shadow as she'd been before. With Matt's love, his belief in her supporting her strong, confident side, she would grow into a more balanced human being. And wasn't that what love was all about? Partners nurturing one another so they were always growing, with each other's help?

Chapter Thirteen

"**I**'m so excited!" Jenny whispered wickedly as she walked arm in arm with Matt toward Morgan's sprawling two-story log cabin. In truth it was a beautiful place that he and Laura had added on to over the years as they had more and more children. Now there was an octagon-shaped living room at one end of the structure. The rest of the cedar home looked more like a standard cabin one would find in the Rocky Mountains of Montana. It was snowing, and she lifted her face to the softly falling flakes as they walked up the recently swept brick path.

Matt grinned. "What about? The Five Days of Christmas party that's going to start tomorrow?"

Jenny was like an exuberant child as she stuck out her tongue and tried to catch the huge snowflakes spiraling lazily downward from the soft gray sky above. He kept his arm around her waist to keep her from slipping.

Smiling up at him, Jenny stopped and threw her arms around his neck. Matt wore a corduroy jacket with a cranberry-red shirt beneath it. Snow lightly covered his short, thick hair. She wasn't disappointed as he lifted her off her feet and captured her smiling mouth.

As they stood kissing hotly on the walk, the silent, mighty Douglas firs like green sentinels around them, Matt eased his mouth from hers—reluctantly. In the weeks since they'd returned home to Montana after the mission, he'd found his life more happy than he could ever believe possible. He had also deferred his upcoming mission in order to spend more time with Jenny. Instead, he had taken over the job as mission planning coordinator and worked with Mike Houston. It gave him the best of all worlds, but more importantly, he had time to be with Jenny to cultivate their deepening relationship.

Now, drinking in her sparkling blue eyes, he gently deposited her on the path.

"What was that sudden, bold attack on me for?" Matt demanded as they turned and began to walk toward the entrance.

"Just because," she answered coyly.

Giving her a skeptical look, Matt grumbled, "When I see that expression on your face, I know I'm in trouble, sweet woman."

Laughing, Jenny stopped and faced him. "The doctor said my sternum is all healed up now, and my ribs are fine. You *know* what that means, I hope?" Her eyes danced with deviltry as she saw his mouth pull into a crooked grin. "Yes, I can see you do!"

"Really?" The last six weeks had been a special hell for both of them. With Jenny's sternum and rib injuries, Matt wasn't about to try and love her, and possibly reinjure her. No, they'd decided to wait until the doctor cleared her. A sweet warmth flowed through him as he saw the glint in Jenny's eyes. How much she'd changed since coming back from Peru. All good changes.

"Really," she murmured. "Come on! We'll be late for the final meeting! There's so much to do for each day of the party!" She grabbed his hand, raced up the steps and opened the ornately carved cedar door. The symbol on it was of the sun and moon entwined with a colorful rainbow. Morgan was the sun. Laura, his moon. And the rainbow, as far as Jenny was concerned, shouted of the love between them and their four beautiful children. She wanted a marriage just like theirs.

Once inside, they shed their coats, hanging them on hooks in the foyer, and removed their boots, placing them on an awaiting rug nearby. Jenny quickly ran her fingers through her blond hair, now damp from the snowflakes. She caught Matt watching her through narrowed, thoughtful eyes. Her body ached to touch him, hold him and love him. The past six weeks had been incredible for her. No longer was she a 'fraidy cat. Morgan liked her new boldness and take-charge attitude. Laura applauded the obvious confidence that she'd brought home from Peru with her. Jenny herself was getting used to this new persona and she liked it—an awful lot. Even better, Matt loved her.

The delicate scent of heated apple juice with cinnamon in it wafted through the cabin as they hurried across the highly polished cedar floor toward the living room, where everyone was to meet. Jenny knew Laura would have cups of the warming cider waiting for everyone.

Christmas music floated through the house, low and joyful. This was Jenny's second year at the five-day celebration that Morgan and Laura threw for all the families of Perseus who lived in Philipsburg. Even better, returning mercenaries were welcome as well. It was five days of nonstop celebration, of making Christmas something special and memorable not only for them, but for the needy, the poor and the sick of the area. Jenny loved it! There was so much fun for everyone, especially the children of the families.

Entering the octagon-shaped room, Jenny spotted everyone cloistered on the thick, comfortable, butter-yellow leather couches that sat in a semicircle around a low oval table made of cedar and glass. Jenny saw red-haired Abbie, a local schoolteacher who was Laura's right-hand woman in decorating for this wonderful event. Next to her sat Colt Hamlin, a mercenary who had just come in off a harrowing mission. Several wives of mercenaries, including Shah Randolph and Susannah Killian were in attendance, as was Sarah Harding, who mined sapphires in the mountains nearby with her mercenary husband, Wolf.

Laura warmly welcomed Jenny and Matt and asked them to come and sit down. She passed around notebooks and pens for all and launched into the coming week's list of activities.

Throughout the two-hour meeting, Matt couldn't keep his mind off Jenny. He had bought a beautiful emerald engagement ring and wanted to ask her to marry him when the time was right. Tonight, he would.

As he sat there, Matt's heart expanded with a love so deep and wide that it made him in awe of the emotion Jenny evoked so easily in him. They'd been living at her condo since they'd come home. Every night, after work, he looked forward to the evenings with her. They made dinner together, then ate it in front of the fireplace, on a soft black alpaca rug she'd brought back from Agua Caliente. More than anything, he enjoyed their deep, exploratory talks. In many ways, Matt thought, the past six weeks had been perfect—a chance for them to get to know one another without sex being a part of their relationship.

Not that he didn't want to love her; he did. But bruised ribs were so very painful; he'd had them once himself. Matt didn't even want to entertain the idea of crushing Jenny with his weight or hurting her by holding her in his arms. The last thing in the world he wanted to do was cause her pain.

Jenny lifted her chin and gazed over at him, a soft smile of welcome on her mouth. He smiled back and caressed her shoulder as she hunched over the notebook and scribbled away. Coordinating this five-day event, Matt was discovering, was like moving an army from point A to point B. Still, he could hardly wait until this meeting was over and they were done for the day. He had a special night planned—for just the two of them.

Slivers of moonlight filtered through the Victorian lace curtains of Jenny's bedroom, where Matt lay waiting for her to emerge from the bathroom. He'd surprised her with a catered dinner, complete with champagne, red roses and a bottle of her favorite perfume, piki-piki, made of white ginger blossoms from Hawaii. It was all part of his telling her he loved her.

The door opened.

His eyes narrowed. Tonight, he had draped the dark green flannel sheet across his hips to hide his lower body, because he wore nothing to bed. Usually, he did, out of respect for Jenny. Tonight, everything was different.

Jenny stood there uncertainly, a fluffy yellow towel wrapped around her. The color complemented her damp blond hair. Her slender hands held the terry-cloth material across her breasts, and she was obviously naked beneath it.

Matt's breath hitched. An ache, so deep and filled with such yearning, flooded his heart and fed his soul as he saw her huge blue, smoky-looking eyes.

Lifting his hand, he murmured, "Come here..." His fingers stretched outward and she moved like a graceful deer, her hand extended toward him. As soon as their fingers touched, he curled her hand into his. Lifting the flannel sheet, Matt guided her into the bed beside him.

"I'm nervous.... I know I shouldn't be, but I am," Jenny whispered. Giving him a pleading look, she added with a twisted smile, "And I'm supposed to have such confidence now because of everything that happened down in Peru."

"You have courage. You always have," Matt said in a rasping tone. Jenny removed the towel and allowed it to drop to the floor, then snuggled beside his long, hard length. "Saving Daniel's life was no little thing, sweet woman," Matt said as he curved his arm around her shoulders and brought her firmly against him.

"I—just feel so inadequate right now," she whispered, closing her eyes and frowning. Matt's body was powerful. More powerful than she had ever realized. As she sank against him, her softness against his granitelike angles, she slid her hand shyly across his flat, hard torso. "I'm worried I won't please you…that my breasts are ugly-looking…or too small…or I won't look good enough for you…." There, the truth was out. Jenny pried her lids open and, risking everything, looked up at Matt.

The tenderness burning in his eyes was her undoing. How could she worry about such things? She saw the love for her reflected in his gaze. And as he moved his hand in a caress across her damp hair, down her cheek to cup her chin, Jenny realized that her anxiety had been for nothing.

A rumble of laughter vibrated within his chest as she met and held his gaze. As her lips parted, Matt guided her chin gently upward and rested his mouth lightly against hers.

"Listen to me, will you?" he whispered across her lips. A hot, throbbing ache centered in his loins, but he ruthlessly controlled it for her sake. "There is nothing ugly about you, Jenny. You're perfect to me. In every way. I'm just as scared, just as worried as you are, sweet woman.''

''You are?'' Jenny's eyes widened enormously as she met and held his smoldering gaze. Shimmering tingles radiated through her, head to toe, as he kept touching her lips like a butterfly, teasing her and letting her know how much he cherished her.

''You see, you aren't the only nervous Nellie around here.'' As Matt's arms moved around her, pulling her against him, Jenny sighed. He was just as scared as she was. He wanted to please her, give her as much pleasure as she wanted to give him. Even though he was a man of the world, a hero in her eyes, he was terribly human—just like her. That evened out the playing field.

Her racing pulse settled a little. The fear that had held her hostage quickly dissolved beneath the exploratory touch of his mouth gliding slickly across her lips. Jenny responded to his tentative kiss, her breath quickening as she pressed herself wantonly against him.

The groan that reverberated through his taut, hard body resonated like a drum within Jenny. As Matt turned and lowered her against the mattress, his arm cushioning her head and shoulders, she closed her eyes and uttered a soft, tremulous sigh. She allowed herself to begin a bold exploration of him, her fingertips trailing languidly from his thick, powerful neck, down across his bunched shoulders to his tense, darkly haired forearms.

"Look at me," he commanded roughly.

His moist breath feathered across her cheek as she slowly opened her eyes. Jenny smiled up into his smoldering, narrowed gaze and saw the love he held for her. Yes, there was no doubt: Matt *did* love her. She saw his mouth curve faintly as he traced her brow with his index finger. There was such tenderness in his expression. Her skin tingled wildly as he move his fingertip downward, across her cheekbone, to the corner of her mouth.

"You are the most beautiful, most precious person in the world to me," he told her in a husky tone as he glided his fingers across her lower lip. "And all I want to do is kiss you senseless and feel myself within you. I've never wanted anyone more than you, Jenny...." And he dipped his head and settled his mouth firmly across her parted lips.

The warm strength of his lips cajoled hers, and a hot fire exploded deep within Jenny's lower body. As he leaned over, pressing her solidly against the mattress, she took his full weight and gloried in his strength as a man. Feeling the rigid hardness of him against her abdomen, Jenny responded boldly by pressing her hips more surely against him. Again Matt groaned. Her heart sang with joy, with the power she had as a woman. His mouth was worshipful against her lips, sometimes teasing, sometimes tempting and always heated and hungry. He wanted her on every level.

Lost in the mindless beauty of the pleasure beginning to throb through her, Jenny felt him tear his mouth from hers. They were both breathing heavily. As his lips settled against the ripe peak of her nipple, Jenny quivered and cried out with pleasure, arching beneath him as he suckled her. Her hands opened and closed in a frenzy as a delicious river of sunlight radiated from her breasts throughout her moving, twisting form.

Helpless beneath his onslaught, Jenny could no longer think. All she could do as he eased one knee between her thighs was to feel herself spiral into a fiery cauldron of desire for him on the most primal, animal level. Sliding her hands over Matt's slick, taut shoulders as he moved across her, she opened her eyes and drowned in his burning gaze. Just as she lifted her hips to meet and meld with him, his entire body momentarily froze.

A low moan of absolute joy slid up her throat as he eased slowly into her tight, slick confines. She felt his arms holding her, cradling her as if she were the most priceless, fragile and beloved being in the universe. There was concern on his perspiring face, and silent questioning in his eyes. Was he hurting her? Was he moving too quickly? Her answer was instantaneous as she arched her hips and drew him deeply, very deeply, within her. Matt hissed, the breath coming between his clenched teeth. Raising his head, he closed his eyes, a grimace making a tortured line of his mouth.

Jenny moaned again as he leaned down and took her lips hotly and commandingly. She felt him thrust into her, a man claiming his woman. There were no words for the sensation, for the powerful movement of his male body against her softer, more giving one. With each rhythmic movement, she felt fire building to a white-hot blaze within her wildly throbbing body. Curling her smaller legs around his massive ones, she clung to him, her face pressed against his sweaty neck. She clung to him with all her womanly strength and felt the cradle of his arms holding and rocking her in an ever-deepening rhythm.

A powerful sensation, like a galactic sun exploding within her, surged and then swept through her, a tidal wave of heat and pleasure. Arching like a bow against him, she released a startled cry of raw gratification. No longer was she the meek, mild Jenny Wright. No, beneath the tutelage, the guidance and supporting love of Matt, she became a woman of wild, primal desire.

Moments spun into a vortex of sun-gold colors, a rainbow of stars shimmering through her sleek, hot body as she climaxed a second and third time in the space of minutes. Matt knew how to please her, how to engage her body and her heart in a way no other man had ever done before. Jenny felt like a violin, her moans of desire and satiation keening out of her throat and whispering from her lips. He played her like a master, her taut body the instrument under his experienced direction.

Jenny felt Matt stiffen. His low animal growl—one of possession, of loving her and making her his in every way—permeated through her. She felt his arms tighten like bands around her, pushing a rush of air out of her lungs. Clinging to him, Jenny realized his life, his love were flowing deep within her welcoming body. Sliding her arms across his torso and arching back, she smiled softly and prolonged his release by moving sinuously against him over and over again.

Finally, he uttered her name and collapsed against her, his head next to hers. Their breathing was labored and chaotic. Jenny kissed his sandpapery jawline, and then his parted lips, and clung to Matt's mouth as he tenderly ravished her in return. His hands moved lovingly across her shoulder, cupping her small breast and then sliding down the line of her hip to her thigh.

"You are so giving," he rasped. Beads of sweat matted his dark hair against his forehead. He felt Jenny's hand move across her cheek to his brow and smooth his hair to one side.

"You are," she said. Then she laughed throatily and met his opening eyes, which were silver with satiation and joy. "I've never felt like I do now, darling. It's you," Jenny whispered, her voice tremulous. Framing his face with her hands, she held his bold, narrowed stare. "I feel like a very rare, beautiful violin that has just been played by a master—you."

Chuckling, Matt eased off her. He didn't want his weight crushing her small form. "A violin?" Rolling to his side, he brought Jenny up against him, one arm behind her neck. With his other hand, he brought up the sheet to their waists. "You're a beautiful woman, Jenny. Beautiful to me in every way."

Her heart fluttered with unparalleled joy. "Really? I wasn't too bad? It was good for you, too?"

Seeing the anxiousness in her eyes, Matt smiled and kissed the tip of her nose. "I feel adored, loved and very, very satisfied, sweet woman." Instantly, he saw all the worry disappear from her huge, blue eyes, which once again danced with gold flecks. As Matt caressed her mussed hair, he smiled down at her. "You're my life, Jenny. You're all I'll ever want or desire. We might have rough times ahead, but just know that through it all, I love you. And together, we'll get through them like the good team we were down in Peru."

Glowing beneath his praise, his heartfelt, rumbling words, Jenny closed her eyes and relaxed against his damp body. His heart was thundering beneath her ear as she pressed her head to his chest. Never had she felt more desired, more loved, than she did now, as he held her in the aftermath.

She felt Matt sigh deeply, the sound coming from his very soul and shuddering out of him. He relaxed with her in his arms. As she opened her eyes, she saw the moonlight shimmering in through the delicate lace curtains and creating a pattern throughout the room. Light and dark. Happy and sad. Joy and grief. Life was all of these things. With Matt at her side, she could weather them all.

"Marry me?"

The words rumbled from him. Jenny's eyes widened. She looked up at Matt. He was studying her tenderly in the moonlight. His wonderfully chiseled mouth curved ruefully as he gazed down at her. She couldn't help but smile in return. Lifting her hand, she moved it against his cheek.

"Yes..."

"You won't be sorry."

"I know...and you won't be, either..."

"I know..." He reached across her and opened the drawer on the bed stand. Fumbling for and finding the ring box, he retrieved it. Easing Jenny upward so that she could lean against him as he rested against the headboard, he placed the small green velvet box in her hand. "Here, this is for you...."

Heart pounding momentarily, Jenny gave him a wide-eyed look and then slowly pried the lid open.

"Oh...Matt!" Jenny looked at the dainty gold ring that had small, rectangular, channel-cut emeralds across it. Even in the moonlight, she could see the stones sparkling as she eased the ring from the box.

Proudly, he watched her expression as she held it up. Jenny was like a child in that moment, amazement written on her face, her well-kissed, softly swollen lips parted in awe. Turning, she met and held his gaze.

"Do you like it?" he asked in a husky voice.

Her face softened. "Like it? I love it, darling." She held it out to him. "Will you?" And she extended her left hand.

How easy it was to slide that engagement ring on her small, slender finger. Matt grinned bashfully as he held her hand and looked at her. "What do you think?"

The corners of her mouth curved upward. She saw the hope, the love, burning in Matt's stormy gaze. Heart bounding wildly, she whispered unsteadily, "Yes...yes, I'll marry you, Matt...."

It took every bit of control he had not to crush her against him. Instead, Matt leaned down and tenderly slid his mouth against hers. As the moonlight bathed them in silent radiance, Matt promised Jenny that he would cherish every moment of life with her from this moment forward—forever.

*　*　*　*　*

*If you loved Jenny's story, you won't want to
miss the next instalment of*

MORGAN'S MERCENARIES

*—Destiny's Woman follows Apache pilot
Akiva Redtail.*

On sale in July 2003 as part of the 3-in-1
Hot Summer Nights.

Only from Silhouette Books.

Here's a sneak preview…

Destiny's Woman
by
Lindsay McKenna

Joe reached over and laid his hand on hers. The moment he touched Akiva, he saw some of the darkness leave her wide, golden eyes. She was so beautiful to him. With her thick black hair down and falling like a cloak around her shoulders, she made him ache to simply hold her and give her that sense of safety she so richly deserved.

Akiva froze inwardly as Joe picked up her hand and held it in his warm, dry one. Every time she talked about the past, she broke into a sweat. It was in reaction, she knew; the past was never far away from her, emotionally speaking. Yet his spontaneous gesture calmed her pounding heart, and she felt her adrenaline dissolving. His touch was magical. Healing. As she stared across the table at Joe, his face alive with anger and pain—sympathy for the pain she'd suffered as a child—something old and dark broke loose within her tightly armored heart.

The moments slowed to a halt between them. She felt her heart opening as his roughened fingers gently caressed hers. The look in his stormy eyes made her feel a thread of happiness that was foreign to her. She *liked* Joe touching her. It made Akiva feel safe. Protected. Hungering for more of that feeling, she stared, confused, into his eyes.

"What's happening?" she asked unsteadily as she looked down at their hands.

"Nothing that isn't good, gal," he whispered rawly. He held her hand up in his larger one. "You deserve some goodness in your life, Akiva. I'm sorry for what happened to you. I can't imagine you, a little nine-year-old girl, going through the kind of hell you just told me about. I wish…well, if I'd been there…"

Warmth and happiness suffused her unexpectedly. Akiva pulled her hand free because she was suddenly frightened by how she was feeling. Wrestling with the happiness throbbing through her chest and warming her lower body, she sat there, hands now beneath the table, folded deep in her lap. The tender flame burning in Joe's gray eyes nearly unstrung her. There was nothing, absolutely nothing, to dislike about this man. And that scared her badly.

Joe knew Akiva didn't trust men in general, and Anglo men in particular. The fact that he was part Indian went a long way in getting her to trust him. Little by little, he felt the walls she held up to keep him out dissolving. It was a heady, scary moment for him. If he said the wrong thing, he knew Akiva would erect those walls again and shut him out once more. That was the last thing he wanted. This was one of the many times Joe felt inept as he floundered mentally and emotionally, casting about for the right words to keep the connection between them alive and strong.

"What we have," he said in a low tone, holding her unsure gaze, "is something special, gal. Something that's being built over time. I like it…whatever it is…and I hope you do, too."

Joe held his breath. He saw Akiva's thin black brows gather. She looked up at the ceiling, as if searching for words. He felt a frisson of fear through his chest. His heart beat a little harder in anxiety.

"Look," he counseled, "don't worry about us, or where this is goin'. We've got a mission and a base to run. That's first. Always first." He watched the play of emotions across Akiva's face. Did she realize how devastatingly beautiful she was?

"Y-yes…the base. And our mission. They always

come first, Joe,'' Akiva replied. She didn't know what else to say. There weren't words to capture the feelings that threatened her control whenever she was with this man....

* * * *

Don't forget Destiny's Woman *is part of the 3-in-1* Hot Summer Nights, *on sale in July 2003.*

▼ SILHOUETTE®
SPECIAL EDITION™

AVAILABLE FROM 20TH JUNE 2003

BUT NOT FOR ME Annette Broadrick

Rachel Wood had never confessed her love to her boss, millionaire Brad Phillips. So why, when she was in danger, did he insist on whisking her to safety—as his convenient wife?

TWO LITTLE SECRETS Linda Randall Wisdom

After a fortnight in the arms of gorgeous Zachary Stone, Ginna Walker sensed that he had a secret he wasn't ready to share. She was sure that she could handle it…but she didn't know that he had *two* little secrets…

MONTANA LAWMAN Allison Leigh

Montana

Librarian Molly Brewster had a new identity…and Deputy Sheriff Holt Tanner had a case to solve. Would his search for the truth force her into hiding—or would his love set her free and make her his?

NICK ALL NIGHT Cheryl St. John

Shock became passion when sexy single dad Nick Sinclair mistook former neighbour Ryanne Whitaker for an intruder! Could his kisses persuade her to swap city life for the warm glow of hearth and home…forever?

MILLIONAIRE IN DISGUISE Jean Brashear

Tycoon Dominic Santorini introduced himself to Lexie only as Nikos—but after an unplanned explosion of desire he couldn't help wondering if she was really a corporate spy. Could he trust the truth he felt in her every touch?

THE PREGNANT BRIDE Crystal Green

Kane's Crossing

Brooding tycoon Nick Cassidy married beautiful Meg Thornton when he learned she was carrying his enemy's baby. The perfect plan for revenge soon turned into love—but would Meg discover the truth?

FREE

4 BOOKS
AND A SURPRISE GIFT!

We would like to take this opportunity to thank you for reading this Silhouette® book by offering you the chance to take FOUR more specially selected titles from the Special Edition™ series absolutely FREE! We're also making this offer to introduce you to the benefits of the Reader Service™ —

★ FREE home delivery
★ FREE monthly Newsletter
★ FREE gifts and competitions
★ Exclusive Reader Service discount
★ Books available before they're in the shops

Accepting these FREE books and gift places you under no obligation to buy; you may cancel at any time, even after receiving your free shipment. Simply complete your details below and return the entire page to the address below. *You don't even need a stamp!*

YES! Please send me 4 free Special Edition books and a surprise gift. I understand that unless you hear from me, I will receive 6 superb new titles every month for just £2.90 each, postage and packing free. I am under no obligation to purchase any books and may cancel my subscription at any time. The free books and gift will be mine to keep in any case.

E3ZED

Ms/Mrs/Miss/Mr ....Initials...
BLOCK CAPITALS PLEASE

Surname..

Address..

....

....Postcode ....

Send this whole page to:
UK: FREEPOST CN81, Croydon, CR9 3WZ
EIRE: PO Box 4546, Kilcock, County Kildare (stamp required)